Ib Svane was born in Copenhagen, Denmark. He was drafted into the Danish army at the age of eighteen and served in the United Nation's forces in Cyprus. He has an academic education from the University of Copenhagen and Göteborg, Sweden, graduating with PhDs in zoology and marine biology. In 1998, he migrated to Australia to work at Flinders University and SARDI Aquatic Sciences in Port Lincoln. During his scientific career, he has published extensively in international scientific journals, popular magazines and elsewhere.

In Cyprus, many people influenced my life and consequently this story. Special thanks to my friends, Rita Mangoian, Avo Mangoian, Erik Flensburg Andersen, and Andreas Demetropoulos. Thanks to Michael Katzev and Robin Piercy for allowing me to dive on the Kyrenia wine ship in the early days of its excavation. My friend, Dr Hans Erik Nielsen, Copenhagen, provided helpful editorial contributions. My lovely wife, Yadranka, was always by my side for which I am grateful.

Ib Svane

THE PEARL OF SAINT-SULPICE

AUSTIN MACAULEY PUBLISHERS™

LONDON • CAMBRIDGE • NEW YORK • SHARJAH

A CIP catalogue record for this title is available from the British Library.

ISBN 9781398470590 (Paperback)
ISBN 9781398470606 (ePub e-book)

www.austinmacauley.com

First Published 2023
Austin Macauley Publishers Ltd®
1 Canada Square
Canary Wharf
London
E14 5AA

I would like to thank Austin Macauley Publishers and the editors for having faith in the story. I am grateful for the tireless efforts of the production team in the face of the Covid pandemic. Without you all, there would not have been any book.

Table of Contents

Prologue   **11**

Part 1: The French Revolution And Before   **15**

1   *17*

2   *19*

3   *24*

4   *26*

5   *31*

6   *35*

7   *39*

8   *46*

Part 2: 1964 and Later   **49**

9   *51*

10   *61*

11   *70*

12   *76*

13   *80*

14	*87*
15	*90*
16	*92*
17	*102*
18	*110*
19	*121*
20	*133*
21	*145*
22	*153*
23	*162*
24	*173*
25	*180*
26	*190*
27	*198*
Part 3: 1974	**203**
28	*205*
29	*208*
30	*217*
31	*222*

Prologue

The genesis of this story is a holy water font in the Church of Saint-Sulpice, Paris. It was made of a shell of the giant clam, Tridacna gigas. I often wondered where it came from because these clams are only found far away from Europe. I find it intriguing that the shell already arrived in France in the early sixteenth century as a gift from the Venetian Republic to King Francis I. Where did it come from? What story could such a shell tell? What thoughts did the sculptor, Jean-Baptiste Pigalle, have when he carved the beautiful column upon which the shell rests? What is its religious significance? Only a few pearls from giant clams are believed to exist and their origins are shrouded in mystery. Is there a pearl somewhere belonging to this clam? It will have to be the Pearl of Saint-Sulpice, alias the Pearl of Allah. But, alas, that pearl and the Pearl of Alexander are products of my imagination.

This story is historical fiction. The framework within which this story unfolds is described as accurately as possible. What I put into words about people, their names and their history in the 15th, 16th, 17th and the 18th century is not fictional but the remainder is. Their actions may not be accurately described because they are only broadly presented in the historical records. The inclusion of The Scarlet

Pimpernel in this story is based on a historical fiction by Baroness Orczy, published in 1905. The Scarlet Pimpernel has, over the years, successfully been transformed into theatre and film enjoyed by many. There is nevertheless an element of truth in the story. Sir William Sidney Smith, his secretary, John Wesley Wright and four royalists did indeed escape from the Temple prison in Paris. They could not have done that without the aid of Sir Percy Blakeney and the French artillery officer, Louis-Edmond Antoine le Picard de Phélippeaux. Phélippeaux and Sidney Smith did play a decisive role in the Battle of Acre after which Phélippeaux sadly died of fever. Sidney Smith described the siege of Acre in The Times, Aug 2, 1799. I admire the bravery of these men.

The cult of Aphrodite is well-known and visitors to romantic Cyprus might be familiar with Aphrodite's temple, birthplace and bath. The magic and the history of the spring at Akamas, Polis, has captivated many people throughout history. I have based the recent tragic history of Cyprus and the events of the Turkish invasion partly on my own experiences. I have freely used sections of the Homeric Hymn to Aphrodite No. 5, translated by Gregory Nagy, the Delphi Complete Dionysiaca of Nonnus by Nonnus Nonnos of Panopolis and the Ode to Aphrodite by Greek poet Sappho also translated by Gregory Nagy. The composer of the Greek rebetiko song *Athenian Girl* is unknown. The speech of Dionysus is partly from the Greek play *The Bacchae* by Euripides, translated by Gilbert Murray.

In my early years in Cyprus, I often visited Kyrenia and Bellapais and spent time in the shade of the Tree of Idleness. With the Concise Oxford Dictionary in my hand (a gift from Rita Mangoian), I laboured through Lawrence Durrell's books, Bitter Lemons and The Alexandria Quartet. I knew exactly where Durrell's house was just up the road but I was neither prepared nor brave enough to knock on his door.

Specialist reading: Svane, I. 1996. Some recent advances in studies on the biology of giant clams (Tridacnidae). Phuket Mar. Biol. Cent. Spec. Publ. No. 16: 221–241.

Part 1
The French Revolution
And Before

1

In 1750, in April, the month of spring, the honourable British Consul at Aleppo, Alexander Drummond, travelled to Aphrodite's Island, Cyprus. On a donkey, he reached his destination, the sacred spring, Fontana Amorosa, Aphrodite's bath. It was here Aphrodite, the goddess of love and beauty, met her lover Adonis. In his travel diary he wrote;

From Buffo, I took my route northwards through the mountains, from some of which I took the bearing to the land about Akamas, where flows the celebrated spring called the Fountain of Love; but I had no curiosity to taste the water, the effect of which upon old people like me, is said to be that of making the spirit willing while the flesh continues weak.

The magical power of the spring had been known for thousands of years. It is the sacred site of pilgrimage of the Aphrodite cult. The only place where Aphrodite's orchid, Serapias aphrodite, grows, empowering the spring helped by the beautiful blue butterfly, Paphos Blue or Glaucopsyke paphos, a native to Cyprus. Little did Alexander Drummond know that from the cliff-tops his every move was closely watched by the Guardians of Aphrodite. Aphrodite is not only the goddess of love and beauty but also war as Homer taught us in his epic story the Iliad from the Trojan War.

The Aphrodite cult in Cyprus has a long history and the concept of female beauty, praised by the ancient Greeks, and later by the Romans is associated with Aphrodite and Venus and their connection to the sea. Aphrodite is like a pearl of the sea. The connection with the Virgin Mary is straight forward. The title "Holy Virgin" is not reserved for her alone but is used for Goddesses like Athena, Asherah, Astarte, Venus, Anat, Ishtar, Diana and others. These Goddesses are also "Love Goddesses", and the ancient meaning of the word "virgin" differs from our modern perception. "Virgin" indicated an independent, autonomous woman, a woman not required to answer to any man. The title had nothing to do with abstinence from sexual intercourse.

This story does not begin here, nor does it end because the story of war, love and beauty is at the infinite mercy of any God.

2

Inside the Church of Saint-Sulpice in Paris, there is an enormous shell of a giant clam given to King Francis I by the Dodge Andrea Gritti of the Venetian Republic in appreciation during the troubled times of the Italian Wars. In the early sixteenth century, the Venetian Republic needed allies and Dodge Gritti was a skilled diplomat seen as a friend of France. In light of threats from northern nations, the so-called princes of the league, whose desire was to extinguish Venice's name entirely, King Francis abandoned his aspirations in Italy and concluded an alliance with the Venetian Republic. One of the Venetian agents told Dodge Gritti, 'King Francis now recognises that the Venetian Republic will never die.'

The French mediator of the treaty was a Sulpician, a monk who was the follower of Sulpitius the Pious's teaching, the late Bishop of Bourges and now a saint, who advocated for priest's education for the good of the society. The Bishop died many years ago but not his teaching. The Sulpicians monks believed that the shell represented divine beauty because in Roman and Greek mythology, Venus and Aphrodite, the goddesses of love and beauty, arose from the sea standing in a giant scallop shell as pure and perfect as a pearl. The monks believed that the giant clam shell was a divine gift from the

Virgin Mary. King Francis I, a well-educated man, agreed with the monks about the divinity of the gift. The king asked the monks to keep the shell under their protection until a church for the Virgin Mary could be built. The giant clam shell was kept safely by the Sulpician monks living and working in Paris. Later the monks formed the Society of Priests of Saint-Sulpice.

In the seventeenth century, nearly 150 years later, the Church of Saint-Sulpice's foundation was laid down in Paris and the first chapel built was La Chapelle de La Vierge, the Lady Chapel or the Virgin Chapel. But it was first during the mid-eighteenth-century that attention was given to the precious gift from the Venetian republic. A famous sculptor, Jean-Baptiste Pigalle, was awarded the commission to sculpture a holy water font using the giant shell. For Jean-Baptiste, this was just a small job. His most significant commission was to sculpt a statue in white marble of the Virgin Mary with Child placed in the chapel's apse.

Jean-Baptiste opened the heavy wooden cask containing the shell and, with the aid of his assistants, placed the shell on a prepared wooden structure, mimicking the natural position as a holy water font. He could now measure the support column's size and carefully draw the art-work that had occupied his mind for some time. Jean-Baptiste envisaged a seabed lifting the shell towards the heavens. He sculptured sea creatures, such as starfish and crabs, into a compelling vision of a cryptic marine environment beneath the clam. It was as if the shell was resting on the surface of the sea; Jean-Baptiste was happy with his work. He left the fine polishing work of the holy water font to his apprentices. Now he could pay attention to the large Virgin Mary statue. Jean-Baptiste looked with delight at a new fresh white marble block ready to be carved. Next to it was a large easel carrying his coal-drawn sketches and a table with chipping tools and hammers of various kinds. He was ready.

His two assistants wanted to move the wooden cask that had carried the shell outside to make space. Before they moved the heavy cask, they had another look to satisfy themselves that they left nothing. An assistant removed loads of packing materials onto a wheelbarrow and carted it outside while the other assistant pulled the remaining material out. In a cry of surprise, he suddenly stopped and looked up. He lifted a heavy leather bag, holding it up in his hands, shouting, 'Monsieur Pigalle, look!' Irritated over the interruption, Jean-Baptiste looked at the assistant and displeasingly uttered, 'Now, what do you have there?' The assistant placed the bag on the tool table and pointed.

'It was on the bottom of the cask.'

Carefully, Jean-Baptiste opened the fragile leather bag, not believing his own eyes. It was a massive elongated pearl of a size and weight he did not think possible. Instantly, he knew it was a natural pearl, nurtured by the clam for many years and eventually appearing as a large irregular smooth block of nacre, starting its journey as a small impurity embedded at the mantle. The size and the lustre was for him a deeply spiritual experience, he at first could not grasp. He thought it must be a divine gift from the Virgin Mary, a holy relic. Without showing his inner feelings, he ordered his assistant to pack it away and place it under the table, indicating nothing of importance. With his keen eye for shape and form, he believed that what he had seen in the pearl was an image, a face, not perfect but a face nevertheless.

He sought guidance in prayers, not talking about the pearl to anyone, intensely fearing the greedy clergy and nobility actions if he told them. Jean-Baptiste believed and accepted that the pearl belongs to the Virgin Mary and should stay with her.

Late in the evening, when the apprentices and the assistants had gone home, Jean-Baptiste lifted the heavy pearl upon the table and took a close look. His eyes had not deceived him; there was a face in the pearl as if someone naively had carved it. He did not know what drove him but he took his tools and started to work on the face without any plan or aim other than to improve what he thought was amateurish and primitive. Slowly, the face of an older man carrying a turban with a mysterious staring look emerged from the pearl giving Jean-Baptiste a mixed feeling of fear and wonder. He stopped carving and began to polish the face. He found the nacre much easier to work on than marble and the face developed from his hands as if it came out of an oil painting he remembered well; a self-portrait by the Dutch master Rembrandt van Rijn. Jean-Baptiste did not know how and why; he just followed his instinct.

He carefully polished the pearl, spending hours to make it perfect and at last he put the pearl aside in its leather bag. That's when he noticed a small folded sheet of waxed paper inside. It had something written and he recognised it as Hebraic, a type of letters he had seen above the entrance to a synagogue. The next morning Jean-Baptiste showed the waxed sheet to one of his apprentices, whom he knew was Jewish, and asked him for a translation. The apprentice looked closely at the text and said, 'I think it is old Hebrew, so I can only make a qualified guess. To get the correct translation, I have to show it to our Rabbi. I guess that the text says;

The Pearl of Allah.

Jean-Baptiste first panicked but then steadied himself. He did not know what to do. Instead, he worked steadily and determinedly on his Virgin Mary sculpture, feeling that the work was his passion, his destiny and only his. Like the pocket at the clam mantel where the pearl was born, Jean-Baptiste carefully carved out a hidden pocket in which he could place the pearl and made a marble plug fitted so accurately the naked eye could not see the delicate interstice. Late at night, he put the pearl in the pocket and sealed the plug. It was now one with the Virgin Mary.

When completed, the sculpture of the Virgin Mary was placed in the Church of Saint-Sulpice, spectacularly located within the Lady Chapel (La Chapelle de La Vierge) under a blue dome in the church's apse.

3

Jean-Baptiste and the Sulpicians, who had guarded the shell and pearl for years, did not know that the Moluccan fisherman, who recovered the pearl, saw the face calling it "The Pearl of Allah". The fisherman hoped that the name would benefit the trading with the Radhanites who had sailed a long way from the Middle East to the Moluccas in South-East Asia to trade for spices.

The Radhanite traders bought the shell and the pearl from the Moluccan fisherman and sailed it to Muscat on the Arabian Peninsula, hoping for a profit. There they showed the pearl to the ruler of Muscat, Azdi Nabahinah. The clan of Azdi Nabahinah was suspicious of the Radhanite traders because they were not Muslims. They had always welcomed them because Muscat prospered from maritime trade. Azdi Nabahinah was impressed and convinced himself that the pearl indeed showed the face of Allah but his clan did not agree. The two parties could not agree on a price but the Radhanites accepted to wait for a decision by the Imam of Muscat, who was due to arrive within a short time after a pilgrimage to Mecca. He was the only one who could determine whether the pearl showed the face of Allah. To the disappointment of the Radhanites, Azdi Nabahinah kept the pearl in the mosque under guard.

But the Radhanite traders had good fortune. The Portuguese Admiral Afonso de Albuquerque arrived with his fleet outside Muscat. He aimed to establish trade relations but the Arabs were so afraid by the fleet's sheer size that they met it with gunfire when the Admiral approached the harbour. He decided to attack the city, which burned down during the fighting. The Portuguese were now in control.

When cannonballs roared over the city, causing destruction and fires everywhere, panic and confusion broke out and many inhabitants fled inland. The Radhanites seized the moment and brought their pearl out of the burning mosque to safety. After the battle, the Portuguese allowed the foreign traders to leave or stay at their wish. The Radhanite traders left and followed their intended route around Yemen and into the Red Sea with their cargo of spices, eventually arriving in the old town of Suez, the gate to the Mediterranean and to their homeland Palestine. Here they sold the shell and the pearl to a Venetian merchant. The Radhanites were now afraid of the pearl and they believed that possessing the Pearl of Allah in Muslim countries would only bring them misfortune. They had a good reason to be afraid. After the Muscat attack, the Imam returned to Mecca and a fatwa was issued stating that the pearl was stolen from the mosque in Muscat, the rightful owner. Now, it was the duty of every Muslim in The Name of Allah to seize the pearl. The Radhanites knew too well that punishment for stealing under Shia Law was the brutal loss of one hand and possibly the head but the shell and the pearl were now in the hands of the Venetians.

4

Jean-Baptiste felt at peace with himself when he had finished the sculpture of the Virgin Mary with Child. When placed in the apse of the chapel, it was admired by many. But his peace did not last long; a fire damaged the chapel badly, discolouring the marble of the sculpture and covering it with ash and soot, making the interstice visible. When he arrived at the chapel to inspect the damage and start the restoration, he was too late. Someone had opened the pocket and the pearl was gone. Jean-Baptiste did neither see the pearl nor his apprentice ever again.

In 1785, at midnight, Jean-Baptiste Pigalle was dying and he called father Jaques Aubert to his death bed. Father Aubert was a Sulpice priest who had known Jean Baptiste for many years and an admirer of the sculptor's work for the church. Father Aubert even believed that God had gifted Jean-Baptiste with an unusual mind and hands, creating such beautiful things with such ease. He was sad when he realised that the great sculptor was dying. When he arrived at Jean-Baptiste's bed, he asked the family to leave so that he could hear the confession alone. Father Aubert talked with the sculptor for a long time, comforting him to face his approaching death.

At last, he asked Jean-Baptiste to confess his sins, preparing him to meet his creator. Jean-Baptiste was silent for a long time, which made the priest nervous. He did not want to see him pass away before a confession. Hesitantly, Jean-Baptiste told his story about the pearl and how he decided to hide it in the sculpture of the Virgin Mary with Child because of his belief that it was a gift from the Lady herself. 'I did not know what happened to me,' he said slowly. 'I had to work on the face and create something better. It told me so. You know, people pray to many of my sculptures and even kiss them. They seem to be the bridge between our physical and spiritual worlds.'

Jean-Baptiste told Father Aubert that his apprentice had translated the name "The Pearl of Allah" from old Hebrew words written on a folded document in the pearl bag. Trembling, Jean-Baptiste pointed to an envelope on his side table. 'You see,' he said with a shivering voice. 'I suddenly realised that I had sculptured the face of God—a mortal sin!'

Jean-Baptiste fell back in his bed, dripping with sweat. He could hardly breathe. He grabbed hold of Father Aubert's hand and continued with a trembling voice, 'Late in the night, I placed the pearl in a pocket carved out in the sculpture of the Virgin Mary with Child. I sealed the pocket with a marble plug and filled the interstice with powdered marble paste. I then polished the surface, leaving no trace at all.'

After a pause, Jean-Baptiste, still holding Father Aubert's hand, said, 'You remember the fire in the chapel? I ran as fast as I could to stop the damage but to no avail. When I arrived, the fire was extinguished but soot was everywhere. To my horror, I saw that the pearl had been removed from the pocket. It had disappeared, most likely along with my Jewish apprentice. There was no trace of him. I searched for him but he was gone. At last, I gave up looking.'

The exhaustion was too much for Jean-Baptiste; he slowly died. Father Aubert prayed for a while. He collected the envelope which contained the folded wax-paper document and a coal drawing Jean-Baptiste had made of the pearl. When Father Aubert arrived back in the Seminar, he made notes of the confession, placed them and the envelope with the drawing in a larger envelope. He sealed the envelope with hot sealing wax with his stamp. Later he archived the envelope in the library of the Seminar.

What father Aubert didn't know was that outside the door, a friend of Jean-Baptiste, a well-established scholar, physician, zoologist and aspiring diplomat, Jean Guillaume Bruguière, was listening. At that time, Paris was facing social and political turmoil leading up to the revolution in 1789. Multiple political groups had clandestine meetings preparing for what to come. Among them, the most influential was the Jacobines of the Jacobin Club. They met regularly at the refectory of the monastery of the Jacobins in Rue Saint-Honoré. Bruguière was familiar with the Venetian gift, protected by the Sulpice monks and was instrumental in awarding the commission for the holy water font to the sculptor, Jean-Baptiste Pigalle. He had often discussed the holy water font with the sculptor but not the pearl the existence of which was not revealed beforehand. For Bruguière, it was a *le jeu politique*, a political game because the clergy involved did not know about the pearl. Still, Bruguière did because of his knowledge and devotion to the study of molluscs. Knowing that it was called "The Pearl of Allah", he found it amusing to discover what the sculptor would do with it. He expected that the pearl would have a dominating role in the holy water font sculpture, supposed to be placed close to the Virgin Mary's statue in the Lady Chapel. Bruguière was disappointed and surprised when he learned that the sculptor had hidden the pearl, showing fear of his own work. He decided to recover the pearl and the opportunity came with the fire. He stored the pearl among his collections in the University of Montpellier in Paris. Bruguière reported his decision to the Jacobines and the Sulpice monks, who had previously approved his actions.

In 1796, the Directoire of the First French Republic wished to find an ally against Russia and decided to despatch two scientists, Jean-Guillaume Bruguières and Guillaume Antoine Oliver, to Persia to negotiate a French-Persian alliance. Bruguières had visited Persia in 1790. He convinced the Directoire that the "The Pearl of Allah" would be a splendid and significant gift to Shahrokh Shah, the Persian king. Bruguières knew that the Shia Muslims of Persia were less inclined to reject images of Allah than their Sunni counterparts in Arabia. He believed that the pearl would be a welcomed holy relic. But his skills as a diplomat was unconvincing and the two scientists soon realised that they could not obtain an agreement. Bruguières played his last card, indicating to the Shah that they, as envoys of the First French Republic, had an important gift, The Pearl of Allah to be presented after a treaty was signed. The Shah asked to see the gift but Bruguières explained that their instruction was not to carry the pearl personally but it would arrive on a French frigate already close to the Strait of Hormuz. The Shah immediately broke the conversation, declaring his displeasure.

A minister announced that Persia was not interested in a treaty with France due to its obligation to the Ottoman Empire.

The two scientists left empty-handed. Bruguières was of ill health and after a stressful voyage the two scientists reached the city of Ancona in Italy where Bruguières died; it was in the year 1798. His friend and colleague brought the Pearl of Allah, alias the Pearl of Saint-Sulpice back to the University of Montpellier. But the mullahs in Qom now knew about the Pearl of Allah and sent a query to Mecca.

5

Not far from the Church of Saint-Sulpice is the École Militaire, a vast complex for military training. It was an institution that could house up to 500 noble young men born without fortune. Here in 1784, Napoleon Bonaparte enlisted at the age of fifteen. One of his contemporaries was a young man, two years older. His name was Louis-Edmond Antoine le Picard de Phélippeaux. It was the time of enlightenment and political discussions among the young noblemen were fierce. Antoine de Phélippeaux was a monarchist while Napoleon was a Corsican nationalist. Napoleons Italian descent affected his language and although he spoke French fluently, it was with an accent. The two men never got along and became fierce competitors, so much that fist-fighting between them was a common occurrence. But Napoleon could never obtain the same quality of performance as Antoine. The two men became enemies for life.

In 1785, the two men graduated from École Militaire. Antoine obtained a commission as Second Lieutenant at an artillery regiment of Besançon and Napoleon also as a second lieutenant but at La Fère artillery regiment. Four years later, Antoine was promoted to Captain but two years later he resigned, escaped the revolution and fled to Great Britain. For four years, he served in Armée de Condé, the Army of Confluence, which had gathered overseas to fight against the French Republic. He returned to France to fight in a royalist insurrection but was arrested and imprisoned in Bourges in central France. Miraculously, he escaped his waiting execution with the help of a relative and secretly joined the counter-revolution outside Paris.

In Britain, Antoine met Sir Percy Blakeney, the leader of the "League of the Scarlet Pimpernel", a secret society of English aristocrats engaging in the rescue of their French counterparts from the Guillotine. Sir Percy and Antoine shared the same aspirations, the fall of the French Republic and the French monarchy's resurrection. Life as a secret agent in France appealed to Antoine and he easily adopted the art of disguise. He frequented a safe house in Rue de l'Université but had many hiding places. In Paris, there was no shortage of supporters willing to help for a small fee.

The two men decided to free an English naval officer, Sir William Sidney Smith, his secretary, John Wesley Wright, and four royalists that had aided Antoine's escape from the Temple prison; a fort built by the Knights Templar in the mid-thirteenth century. It was the same prison that had earlier housed the French royal family before their execution. Antoine knew from his military studies that the Templar had constructed a tunnel from the Master of France's house to the great tower's dungeon. With the help of a mason and unseen by the guards, the two men located the entrance to the tunnel. But to no avail the tunnel was filled with water and closed with rocks at the dungeon. Now their situation was dire and the time of execution was fast approaching.

Much to Sir Percy's amusement, Antoine, disguised as a gardener, charmed the jailer's daughter. She could not resist his advances and gentlemanly behaviour, giving her gifts of flowers, perfume and small jewellery. They became lovers and secured communication with the prisoners. Meanwhile, the royalist's procured false papers. When a generous gift of wine that incapacitated the jailer, Antoine and Sir Percy presented themselves at the gate as police commissionaires with a forged order of release. Sir William Sidney Smith and the others were quickly whisked out of prison and into a waiting carriage. The driver drove the carriage at great speed into the street. But before long, the forgery and the escape was discovered. A group of prison guards were quickly in pursuit. The carriage driver did his best to get away but the carriage overturned at a sharp turn and within long a crowd had gathered. Antoine used to command men, forced himself, Sir Pierce and the escapees through the public. In darkness, the group proceeded on foot through Paris's streets and arrived safely at a safe house in rue de l'Université.

The same night, a person arrived at the safe house with a heavy package. It was Pierre-Simon de Laplace. He was Antonie's and Napoleon's teacher and examiner at Le École Militaire. His outstanding teaching at Le École Militaire and the university had given him freedom during the early years of the revolution. He brought the Pearl of Allah, alias the Pearl of Saint-Sulpice, secured at the University of Montpellier by Guillaume Antoine Oliver with the instruction to under Antonie's guardianship carrying the pearl to Britain until the turmoil in France subsides. After delivering the package, Pierre-Simone swiftly disappeared into the darkness of the streets.

The following morning, Antoine, Sir Percy and the five men found a path to the coast at Rouen, where a royalist was waiting with a set of forged passports. The group quickly dressed in sailor clothes and travelled to Honfleur, a fishing town where the Seine River meets the English Channel. A small fishing boat was waiting, taking the company out in the channel to meet a waiting British ship. When news about the daring rescue arrived in the London high society, there was a relief and when Sir William told others, Antoine or Phélippeaux as his British friends called him, became a hero. Sir Percy denied any involvement, stating that he had been hunting foxes on his Kent estate.

6

Admiral Nelson was basking in his reputation as a hero of the Battle of the Nile, where he destroyed a French fleet in August 1798. He was now convalescing from his wounds in the arms of Lady Hamilton in Naples. Much to his annoyance, the eager young Sidney Smith has attracted the Admiralty's attention and was appointed Commodore of a flotilla in the Eastern-Mediterranean under Lord St Vincent's command. He was the captain of HMS Tigre, a captured 80-gun French ship of the line and had the authority to take British ships under his command.

Napoleon's defeat at the Nile had left him stranded and, to some degree, curtailed his ambition to be the master of the Levant (the Middle East) to join Tipu Sultan, the Tiger of Mysore fighting the British expansion in India. The First French Republic's Directory has sanctioned his conquest of Egypt, which would give them a foothold in the Middle-East and free the enslaved people of the Ottoman Empire. The young Bonaparte was getting too popular for the Directory. Importantly, Napoleon had the army's support. The Directory was delighted to see him off to be someone else's headache.

Napoleon pushed on and marched his troops across Sinai and laid siege to Jaffa, defended by the Ottomans led by Pasha al-Jazzar. Napoleon sent messengers to the Pasha, ordering him to surrender. He did not but instead, the messengers were decapitated and their heads impaled on the city walls. This act infuriated Napoleon and after successfully breaching the defences, he executed more than 3000 prisoners, most of them Albanians. Napoleon did not have the luxury to take prisoners or let them go because they would probably swell the ranks of al-Jazzar's troops.

After his success at Jaffa, Napoleon pushed on to Acre, a strategically located city controlling the coastal road and the road through the Jezreel Valley leading to Damascus.

Sidney-Smith had invited his friend, Antoine Phélippeaux, who had gained a British Colonelcy, to join him on a diplomatic mission to Constantinople to meet the Ottoman ruler, Selim III. After that, they sailed to Acre to help the commander Pasha al-Jezzar against the French forces. It was now Phélippeaux job to assist the Pasha with the defence of Acre. As a trained artillery officer, Phélippeaux quickly realised that the medieval fortifications were in a poor state of decay and quickly needed improvements. He had the confidence of the Pasha and large gangs of labourers where provided under his command. It did not take long before Phélippeaux had strengthened the walls and excavated the moat filled through years of neglect. He dug trenches and build walls behind the old fortifications, making it difficult for the attacker and easy for the defenders. He installed cannons at strategically important places. As good luck, Sidney-Smith had intercepted barges loaded with light cannons and ammunition, destined for Napoleon's troops to be used at the siege.

On March 20, the siege began with attacks of the French infantry. Sidney-Smith had anchored his two ships, the Tigre and the Theseus, to assist Ottoman-British gunboats shelling the coastal road preventing the infantry from reaching the fortifications. A month later, Napoleon received a replacement for the lost artillery and forced a breach in the Acre defences. It was man-to-man combat led by Phélippeaux and al-Jazzar's Jewish adviser and right-hand man, Haim Farhi.

Antoine Phélippeaux had brought with him his secret possession, the Pearl of Saint-Sulpice or the Pearl of Allah. During conversations and dinners with the military leaders of Acre and the commander Pasha al-Jazzar, Phélippeaux had told the history of the holy water fond at Saint-Sulpice and the pearl. He told them that the pearl showed an image of a man, which some believed was God or Allah's. The Pasha thought that he had heard a similar story of a pearl that arrived in Muscat with Radhanite merchants and offered for sale. He warned Phélippeaux that a fatwa had been issued in Mecca more than 200 years ago, claiming the pearl for the mosque in Muscat, a never solved dispute. The officers found the story amusing but before long, the rumours of the Pearl of Allah's presence spread among the superstitious troops inside the walls.

At the height of the battle, Napoleon's infantry had managed to gain a foothold in the wall's breach. Quickly, an avalanche of troops flooded through to be met by fire from the defenders in trenches. At that point, Phélippeaux realised that something extraordinary had to happen to prevent further influx of French troops. He quickly dispatched his assistant to fetch the bag with the pearl. When the French forces were rampaging through the breach, Phélippeaux bravely got up on the rampart, ignoring the bullets, facing his troops holding the pearl towards them, shouting, 'Look at the Pearl of Allah. Allah is with us!' He handed the pearl to his assistant and, with his raised sword in his hand, stormed towards the French intruders screaming, 'In the name of Allah, attack, attack!' A gigantic roar came from the Ottoman troops who fiercely followed Phélippeaux's attack and threw themselves against the French. The sudden outburst of the massive sound of hundreds of screams and fighters sacrificingly throwing themselves on the attackers, forcing the French troops backwards in panic, leaving scores of dead behind them. Covered in blood, Phélippeaux stood breathless among his troops watching the remaining French withdrawing in scrambles down the rampart.

Not long after the victory at the siege of Acre, Phélippeaux died in fever. He was only 31 years old. When Napoleon wrote his memoirs exiled on St. Helena in the South Atlantic Ocean, he accepted that the two men, Antoine Le Picard de Phélippeaux and Sir William Sidney Smith, had made him miss his destiny. 'Without them, I would have taken the key to the Orient; I would have marched on Constantinople; I would rebuild the throne of the Orient.' Now, the Pearl of Saint-Sulpice was under the protection of Phélippeaux's assistant in a foreign land.

7

As soon as Al-Jazzar heard the news that the breach of the city's defence had been repelled decisively under the courageous leadership of Phélippeaux and Haim Farhi, he was delighted. But when he heard that Phélippeaux had raised the Pearl of Allah as a heraldry encouraging the heroic counterattack, he immediately decided to despatch an envoy to Mecca to obtain written confirmation of the fatwa and its argument. The Pasha might have chosen to seize the pearl straight away but he was wise enough not to upset his British alley.

Napoleon had brought scientists with him to Egypt and their most outstanding achievement was the finding of the "Rosetta Stone". A young Lieutenant, Napoleon's aides-de-camp Pierre-François Bouchard, found the stone while repairing an Ottoman Fort, Fort Rashid, a few kilometres before the River Nile joins the Mediterranean Sea. The finding of a stone with hieroglyphs may not be unusual but the critical feat was to recognise its importance. The scientists soon realised that the stone carried three pieces of inscribed text, a hieroglyphic and a Demotic text, both of Egyptian origin and a translation into ancient Greek. For many years, scholars had tried to understand the meaning of hieroglyphs.

Now, it was in front of their feet. For Napoleon's ambitions, it was of little importance. He may have inadvertently found the key to understanding ancient Egypt but he did not find a Rosetta Stone or key to unite the Jews and the Muslims to rise against their Ottoman Ruler. But Napoleon was a shrewd politician. He attempted double play and claimed that he had not come to the Middle East to destroy Islam but to restore their rights and punish the usurpers. To the Egyptian people, Napoleon declared, 'I respect God, his Prophet and the Quran. Is it not we who have been through the centuries the friends of the Sultan?'

During the siege of Acre, Napoleon published a proclamation in which he invited all the Jews of Asia and Africa to gather under his flag and re-establish the ancient Jerusalem. He spread rumours among Syrian Jews that he would go to Jerusalem and restore Solomon's temple after his conquest of Acre. This rumour would become an early avant-courier for the Zionist movement. In Acre, his message was intended for al-Jazzar's Jewish adviser and confidant, Haim Farhi, trying to persuade him to betray his master. But he was not convinced and fought bravely alongside Phélippeaux.

When Haim Farhi learned that Phélippeaux had come down with fewer, he immediately went to his quarters, bringing along the military surgeon, also of Jewish descent. Haim Farhi realised that Phélippeaux was not likely to survive the fever, which had already killed many soldiers. He decided to seize the Pearl of Saint-Sulpice alias the Pearl of Allah and bring it to Constantinople, safely out of reach of his Muslim ruler. He had experienced the power of the pearl and could not allow it to be used against his people. The military surgeon removed the bag with the pearl from Phélippeaux belongings and replaced it with a fake bag containing a stone of similar weight.

After Phélippeaux's death and funeral in Acre, his assistant boarded HMS Tigre under Commodore Sir William Sidney Smith's command and left for Egypt.

The night Phélippeaux died, the pearl was carried by a Marrano Jew, a diplomat of the Ottoman Empire, on an Ottoman galleon en route to Constantinople via Cyprus. When the envoy to Mecca returned, HMS Tigre and the Ottoman galleon were way out at sea.

Not long after their departure from Acre, Sidney Smith and Phélippeaux's assistant discovered that the pearl was replaced by a stone. Both men felt deep despair but Sidney Smith's experience as a spy and secret agent took over. He concluded that the thief could not be Al-Jazzar because he was waiting for his envoy to return from Mecca. 'A likely candidate could be the Jewish surgeon because he was the only one in Phélippeaux's quarters except for Haim Farhi,' Sidney Smith explained to the assistant.

'We have to inform Pierre-Simon Laplace, who in Paris came with the pearl and at once reveal our suspicion and request a drawing of the pearl.' Without explaining more, the Commodore jumped up and immediately wrote a coded letter to be despatched to France via one of his agents among Napoleon's officers.

The coded letter arrived in Laplace's office in Paris in November 1799, shortly after Napoleon had seized power in the bloodless coup d'état, the Coup of 18 Brumaire, which ended the revolution. Napoleon was now the First Consul of France and appointed his teacher at Le École Militaire to be Minister of Interior. It did not take long before Laplace contacted the Society of the Priest of Saint-Sulpice. The Society provided the drawing that the sculptor, Jean-Baptiste Pigalle, had given to the priest, Father Aubert, during his confession shortly before his death. The Church of Saint-Sulpice had a special place in Laplace's heart because in 1788, at the age of 39, he was married in the church to the eighteen-year-old Marie-Charlotte de Courty de Romanges.

Pierre-Simone Laplace was in Napoleon eyes, not the administrator he expected and after just six weeks in the job, Napoleon dismissed him and gave the post to his own brother. But Laplace was a formidable physicist, mathematician and philosopher equal to Isaac Newton. In public, he was not too concerned about politics and carefully navigated through the revolution's turbulent times and Napoleon's reign. After the fall of the empire, Laplace found his rightful place in French society. During the restoration of the Bourbon monarchy, he was honoured with the title of Marquis.

When the Ottoman galleon arrived at the port of Famagusta on the East coast of Cyprus, the diplomat immediately walked to the Synagogue. The diplomate's name was Solayman Hamadani, born in Persia by Jewish parents. His parents had deliberately given him a Persian name to hide his Jewish origin. He considered himself a Marrano Jew, devoted to crypto-Judaism. By day, he would pray in the mosque and by night he would meet with fellow Jews to practise his genuine faith, Judaism. During the Ottoman rule, Jews were not persecuted. It was not unusual for a diplomat to visit the Synagogue in Famagusta, where more than 2000 people of Jewish descent lived. It happened to be that the Rabbi in Famagusta was his uncle. His mission was to persuade his uncle to be the Pearl of Allah's keeper until he could find a safer place.

Together the two men studied the pearl, which made a deep impression on the Rabbi. It was easy for him to read the old Hebrew text stating that the pearl was indeed The Pearl of Allah. Based on the writing style, the Rabbi inferred that it must have been brought to the Middle East by the Radhanites, Jewish merchants who frequently travelled to South-East Asia and as far as China long before Marco Polo. 'But I think,' he said in deep thoughts, 'that the image of a man's face is not natural to the pearl but carved by a skilful artist.' Hamadani agreed and eventually asked the difficult question of whether the Rabbi could house the pearl until he found a more permanent place for it.

The Rabbi got up and looked carefully through the window. People and carts with goods were passing in the street outside. He ensured himself that nobody was observing the house and rang a small bell with a wooden handle. Soon after a servant appeared and he and the Rabbi exchanged a few words. The servant disappeared down the corridor and out through a heavy door mingling with people in the street. The Rabbi turned towards his nephew and slowly said, 'I am worried; how do you know that you have not been followed, the pearl is not of trivial importance and value.'

Hamadani thought for a while and said, 'I don't think anybody followed me. Pasha Al-Jazzar cannot have communicated with his agents before I arrived in Famagusta but he is likely to have people on the galleon. When I left, the Pasha was waiting for an envoy to return from Mecca. If the Pasha has agents on the galleon, Haim Farhi would know and would have warned me.'

The Rabbi looked worried at Hamadani, opened a drawer in his desk and fetched a large thick sealed envelope and handed it to his nephew. 'We better make this meeting official and formal. Will you please bring these documents to Constantinople and in-person deliver them to the Hakham Bashi, the official Government-appointed Chief Rabbi of important cities in the Ottoman Empire—my servant will escort you back to the galleon.' As soon as Hamadani had left, the Rabbi located a small hole between the polished lime stones in the wall. He pushed a thin iron rod into the hole and a floor tile below slowly slid under the limestone wall, revealing a space big enough to contain the pearl in its bag and much more. The Rabbi took the thin iron rod and pushed it into another hole. The tile came out from the wall and sealed the space below.

When Al-Jazzar's envoy arrived from Mecca, confirming that indeed a fatwa had been issued claiming ownership of the Pearl of Allah on behalf of the mosque in Muscat, he was furious. His fury was not about the potential value of the pearl or the effect it had on his superstitious subordinates but the missed opportunity. His successful defence of Acre against Napoleon Bonaparte's forces, disregarding the vital support of the British navy had earned him prestige in the Ottoman Empire. He was now well-known in Europe. *Al-Jazzar knew that bringing the Pearl of Allah to Mecca and thereby end the fatwa would give him prestige within the Muslim world. He had been denied this honour just because of his misplaced respect for the British*, he thought. *But soon, his role as Governor of Damascus kept him busy.*

Ahmad Pasha Al-Jazzar was a dangerous man and the thought of the missed opportunity with the Pearl of Allah did never leave him. He knew too well that his name, Al-Jazzar, means "the Butcher", an epithet he earned for a deadly ambush on Bedouin tribesmen in retaliation for a Bedouin raid that killed his master. He was also known as a skilled assassin when he was in the service of Egypt's ruler, Ali Bey Al-Kabir. His contemporaries knew that crossing Al-Jazzar's path could have serious consequences. He did not think of the possibility that Al-Jazzar's Jewish adviser and right-hand man Haim Farhi was involved. *What interest could he has in a Muslim pearl,* he thought. He concluded that it was the British assistant who had taken his masters pearl with him and for now, he could not do anything about it. His dream of housing the Pearl of Allah in his newly built Al-Jazzar Mosque in Acre had evaporated.

After Napoleon's fall, the Ottoman Empire was in relative peace and prosperity, including Cyprus, which experienced a high degree of autonomy under the Cypriot Orthodox Church's governance as an independent mutasarrifate. It ended in 1878 when Cyprus came under British rule during the Russo-Turkish War. During that time and further on, the Pearl of Saint-Sulpice, alias the Pearl of Allah, was believed to remain safely under the Synagogue's floor in Famagusta.

8

Before and during the French revolution, the leader or Superior General of the Society of Priests of Saint-Sulpice was a man of authority, Father Jacques-André Emery. He was a canon lawyer with the desire and capacity to reform the Seminary of Paris, which had declined over many years. The unwelcome arrival of the revolution changed his plans because the National Assembly voted in favour of "the Civil Constitution for the Clergy" in 1790, approved by King Louis XVI now a marionette. Father Emery realised with fear that this law provided a revolutionary tool to divide the church. His principle was clear; the church had to remain tied to the Bishop of Rome and this principle could not be called into question. But the challenges to the priests of Saint-Sulpice were immense. Catholic priests everywhere were in danger; the Reign of Terror had begun. In 1773, the self-established National Convention enacted the Law of Suspects. It declared that anyone considered to be a counterrevolutionary was guilty of treason and an enemy of the Republic. There was only one verdict; being sentenced to death by the guillotine. Thousands of people were executed to the entertainment of the mob or proletariat, who gathered at the guillotines set up in Paris and places elsewhere in France. Among the executed were many Sulpice priests. Those who survived had fled overseas.

Father Emery escaped the Guillotine by cunningly supporting a group of radical members in the National Assembly, the Jacobines. But his fear of the Conciergerie, where the Revolutionary Tribunal issued arrest orders at the whim of the feared prosecutor, was ever-present. The Society of the Priests of Saint-Sulpice had already been established in Montreal and Baltimore. Father Emery dispatched four members of the society to Baltimore and wrote a letter to the first superior, expressing his fear that the society was in great danger of being extinguished in France. The only possibility was to re-establish the society in America. Father Emery decided to recover the Pearl of Saint-Sulpice from the University of Montpellier, expecting it to be kept by the entomologist and naturalist Guillaume-Antoine Olivera, who had brought it back from his and Jean Guillaume Bruguiére's unsuccessful mission to Persia.

It was dangerous times but Father Emery send a trusted priest in disguise to Montpellier, requesting the pearl to be brought to the Seminar. The priest returned empty-handed with the information that the pearl was in a secure place under Pierre-Simone Laplace's supervision, who was no longer in Paris. Father Emery was furious but could not do anything to retrieve the pearl to the Priest of Saint-Sulpice's benefit. He nevertheless wrote a document that officially transferred the Pearl of Saint-Sulpice's ownership, alias the Pearl of Allah, to the society of the Priests of Saint-Sulpice in Baltimore. He requested the Superior General to find an appropriate location for the pearl in the newly built Mary Chapel at the Seminar in Baltimore. Later, Father Emery learned that the pearl was present at the Battle of Acre in Palestine and communicated his information to Baltimore.

In London, a small group of Sulpicians, refugees from the French Revolution, had built a chapel dedicated to the Annunciation. Their life and devotion gained respect from the Anglicans, who left the Sulpicians alone. When Napoleon took power, making Paris a more peaceful place, Father Emery wrote to the Sulpice priests in London requesting information about the whereabouts of the pearl because he believed that it was in the hands of the British, considering the role the pearl played in the Battle of Acre. The answer from the Sulpicians in London came months later. They promised to keep their eyes and ears open and to make enquiries when appropriate. It was not the answer Father Emery had hoped.

Part 2
1964 and Later

9

On the North-Western coast of Brittany, France, 60 kilometres east of Brest is a town called Roscoff. It's a busy ferry harbour connecting France to the city of Cork on the Irish south coast and British harbours along the Channel coast. Many tourists are visiting the town and the port, which has a significant tidal range. Lobster and crab fishers set their traps and nets at neap tide because, at spring tide the currents are so strong that both nets and traps can be carried away or fouled with drifting algae. The fishing boats leave the harbour at the outgoing tide when there is enough water depth to lift their keels above the bottom. The boats return at high tide but it is a race against time. At low tide, the harbour is dry and they all have to come in before the tide leaves no water below the keel. If late, the boats have to wait for the next incoming tide about 6 hours later. The late-comers have to face the harbour wall while standing on the bottom. It's a long way up to the truck loading bins of lobsters and crabs for the fish market. Offloading the catch is less laborious at high tide.

In Roscoff, there is a marine laboratory belonging to the University of Sorbonne in Paris. It is called Station Biologique de Roscoff and has been there since 1872. It's a famous laboratory visited by many marine scientists from around the world. Scientists can collect animals and algae at low tide and work with the collected material in the laboratories. The station has a dormitory for the scientists and their students.

In a separate building is an impressive library containing many scientific books and journals. The librarian was a quiet French lady who rarely spoke to anyone away from the library. For years, she had been living in one room in the dormitory, raising two children. She always left her room in the middle of the night, carrying a bucket and two rolls of paper and walked the cobblestone streets towards the town centre. She kept away from the lights at a distance looking like a shadow. Then she stopped, put her bucket on the ground and folded out one of the paper rolls. It was posters. She quickly covered the back with glue and fixed it to the wall using a broad brush. She affixed her placards on all the public places; they were all propaganda for the French Communist Party. By two in the morning, she was back in her room. It was a daily routine not questioned by anyone. The following day, council workers removed the librarian's posters. This tuck-of-war had been going on for a long time. The revolutionaries in France still have aspirations, although their numbers were in decline.

In Roscoff, you can feel the cold air from the sea travelling up the cobblestoned streets with the incoming tide. Many times it is followed by dense fog and the mournful sound of foghorns further away. When ships had no radar or other equipment to determine where the coast and reefs were, they would stay far away. Sailors would carefully listen to the foghorns and to the sound of breaking waves.

The lecture theatre at Station Biologique de Roscoff was filled with marine biology students. They were not the only ones; among them were several lecturers and people from most biology departments in the museum and Paris universities. The station had a guest, a specialist in mollusc bivalves, who had travelled from the United Kingdom to present his work. It was the first time he was here because he had spent most of his career studying a particular group of bivalves found on the Great Barrier reef of Australia, stretching hundreds of kilometres along the Queensland coast. In particular, one genus, the giant clams, is found abundantly on the reef. They can be found elsewhere in South-East Asia, such as southern Philippines, Indonesia and even at the Andaman Islands in the Gulf of Bengal. But outside the Great Barrier Reef, the largest one, Tridacna gigas, weighing more than 400 kilograms at a length of about 140 centimetres and reaching an age of 100 years or more, is rare; out-fished by humans, who could find them easily in the warm shallow reefs. There are similar clams, but relatively smaller, distributed all over South-East Asian and the western Pacific, even in the Red Sea, far away.

The professor entered the podium, organised his notes and looked up. The silence was deafening, keeping the audience in a state of excited expectation. He began, 'The Latin name of the genus is Tridacna from the Greek word, tridaknos, meaning eaten in three bites, coined in a joyful moment by the 18th-century naturalist Jean-Guillaume Bruguières. When Captain Cook visited the Great Barrier Reef and saw with amazement the large clams, he wrote in his journal:

Cockles, of so enormous a size, that one of them was more than two men could eat. The demise of the giant clams is due to their sweet flesh so easily and thoughtlessly obtained. Giant clams have been here for more than 200 million years, quietly filtering plankton from the water. But they are not defenceless. There are sensors in their mantel, activated by prodding intruders and eyespots sensitive enough to register a passing shadow. Instantly, in a sudden movement, the clam will close its shell a few inches with an audible sound followed by a jet of water, precisely and forcefully expelled from the exhalent siphon directed against any intruder.'

The professor looked up and pointed at a jug of water and glasses out of his reach. A student on the first row jumped up, grabbed the jug and glass and served water for the professor, who swallowed the glass's content in one slurp. His eyes returned to his notes and he continued, 'Apart from their size and a maximum weight of 800 to 900 pounds, what is remarkable is the colour of the mantle and their mesmerising symbiosis with zooxanthella. It is these colours that captivate us when snorkelling next to a giant clam. We rarely see the symbionts, a type of dinoflagellate because they hide in the mantle's ciliated channels. The colours we see are not just to entertain the observer but also essential for the clam's survival. During evolution, the clams have developed pigmentation protecting them against harmful wavelengths of light. Still, not surprisingly, the pigmentation ensures that only the optimal light frequency will reach the zooxanthellae.'

The professor drank another glass of water while his assistant showed colourful photographic slides of the mantle of several species of giant clams. He looked out in the lecture theatre with a satisfying smile when he heard sighs of amazement. An old wall clock ensured him that he had not wasted more time than necessary. He continued, 'It is the so-called iridophores that provide the colours. Iridophores give rise to an almost infinite variety of brilliant colour patterns, especially in the smaller species. Each iridocyte contains a laminated body composed of flattened platelets. The iridocytes occupy the same region of the clam's mantle as the photo synthetically active zooxanthellae, confined in a narrow tubular system as I mentioned previously. I will not discuss this system further but mention another type of iridophore found in the heart clam, Corculum cardissa, which also possesses zooxanthellae. You see, there are ample opportunities for those of you who want to "Assume the Mantle" so to speak and study these remarkable animals further.'

'Now, let's get to the important points,' the professor emphasised, convincing himself that he was on the right track after having observed yawning by people on the back rows. 'The symbiotic zooxanthellae in giant clams are similar across the range of host animals and therefore not unique. Several theories are put forward on how they are acquired. Still, it is generally accepted that they enter the animal unharmed via the digestive system and leave extruded in faecal pellets.' The professor paused, took a deep breath and continued, 'In my previous work I believed that the zooxanthellae were maintained intra-cellular in blood amoebocytes located in the haemal sinuses of the siphonal tissues where they were periodically digested and accumulated as concretions in the enlarged kidney. Regrettably, I was wrong. It is now evident that an elaborated tubular system is connecting the siphonal tissue with the stomach. More regrettable, I wrongfully rejected the early work by the Egyptian scientist, Dr K. Bashour, who after the war had submitted a paper on this subject to "Nature". The criticism in my review unintentionally prevented further studies.'

Something happened to the professor. His face changed colour from boiling red to white. He grabbed after the glass he had already emptied, looked at the audience while his body slowly slipped behind the podium. The only thing visible to the audience was his feet sticking out. Panic evolved but within minutes someone lifted him in a chair and placed a bag of ice on his head. Everybody in the lecture theatre was watching in silence until a comment was heard, 'Bloody arrogant pom, I can imagine what he had done to the poor Egyptian; he probably ended his career. I am surprised that he had to eat that one!' Then somebody shouted, 'Coffee break! ' and the audience dispersed out in the corridor. A middle-aged man of olive complexion got up and walked to the corridor for a coffee. His name was Kamal Bashour. He came from Egypt.

Half-an-hour later, the lecture theatre was again full of spectators waiting with excitement. The professor was not well and still kept an ice-bag on his head. Despite encouragements from the organisers of the meeting, the professor refused to leave. Then it was announced that Professor Junge from the Marine Biological Association in Plymouth was postponing his lecture until tomorrow. Instead, Dr Kamal Bashour from the University of Cairo will present his talk on giant clams' physiology.

Kamal Bashour nervously entered the podium. He had never given a lecture outside Egypt and felt that his English language might irritate some in the audience. He was fluent in French and of course in Arabic and Coptic Egyptian. He could travel to France and participate in the meeting because of a generous stipend from the French government, recommended by the French Academy of Science.

On the podium, Kamal looked at his lecture notes and decided to ignore them. He thought that his English scribbles would confuse him. He looked nervously at the audience but quickly gained his composure and spoke with authority. 'The weight of the viscera of a giant clam is too much to be sustained by filter-feeding alone. A source of energy has to come from somewhere else. It is here the zooxanthellae play an important role. In culture, the zooxanthellae assimilate carbon at similar rates as free-living dinoflagellates but in symbiosis, a substantial part of the carbon is taken up by the host. However, the key to understanding the symbiosis is that the photosynthesis rate varies as a function of the inorganic carbon concentration of the haemolymph, which is in equilibrium with the surrounding seawater. The limiting factor for the zooxanthella is the enzyme carbonic anhydrase level on the external cell membrane. My studies have shown that the highest concentration of the enzyme carbonic anhydrase is found in mantle extracts associated with the zooxanthella tubes in the mantle as I described in my paper in Nature in 1946.' Kamal looked at Professor Junge, who was now laying down across four seats, still with an ice bag on his head dreaming about the blood amoebocytes that never were. Kamal continued, 'It is now clear that the clam provides carbonic anhydrase to the zooxanthellae to facilitate uptake of

CO_2 and furthermore, supply nutrients in the form of ammonium, nitrate and phosphate. In return, the zooxanthellae provide glucose easily absorbed by the mantle tissue, explaining why giant clams become larger than other clams.' Dr Kamal Bashour looked out in the audience, feeling more confident as his adrenaline levels became exhausted. Professor Junge did not move or say anything when the chair asked for questions from the audience. After a serious discussion of the subject, the meeting was closed to be convened the following day.

Later in the evening, Professor Martin Junge and the laboratory director, Pierre Le Barré, had dinner together. To make it easy, they decided to have their evening meal in a basement restaurant across from the laboratory, frequently visited by the station's scientists. The restaurant was a simple operation. There were the chef and his assistant, a young lady. Tables and benches were along the wall and in the middle of the room was a cooking island. Along another wall was a large fridge with glass doors. It was a fixed menu, new every day and the chef was cooking the food while his customers were watching. There were many guests, particularly the participants from the meeting. The Director, Pierre Le Barré, had wisely booked a table, so the two academics easily slipped into a somewhat secluded table out of hearing from the noisy crowd. It was customary on busy nights that patrons had to wait in an adjacent small room and were offered a free drink. After their drink, they were escorted to a table, sat down and ordered water and wine. The assistant restaurateur placed a cheese platter in front of them. She poured the wine and quickly the cheese platter disappeared to another table. Disappointed, the two men look in the direction of the disappearing plate. Le Barré laughed and explained that in this restaurant, you have to be fast. But the two gentlemen knew that the food was excellent and in the classical French tradition.

'You know, Pierre,' Martin Junge said, 'tomorrow we have a new guest who will make an announcement. His name is Alexander William Sidney Smith, the great-great-grandson of Admiral William Sidney Smith. He fought so brilliantly in the Napoleonic wars but more importantly, he played a vital role for the Royalist France as a spy. Alexander is now a captain in the Royal British Navy.' Martin Junge was silent for a while, looking at Pierre Le Barré. Pierre nodded in agreement. Martin Junge looked around and took a sip of his wine. Pierre Le Barré was warming a glass of cognac. 'You know,' Martin continued, 'MI5 has decided to put effort into looking for the Pearl of Saint-Sulpice yet again after a request from your people. They have sent Alex to give a presentation as a representative of The Royal Society of London. As you know, there are other players in this game and I am a little worried about the presence of the Egyptian, Kamal Bashour. My people have shrouded off any of my concerns but I am still worried. We have to be cautious.'

Pierre Le Barré nodded again and added in a low voice, 'I agree.'

'We have had a close look at the pearl called The Pearl of Allah, which was recently found, probably in the Philippines, currently locked up in a bank vault in the US.' Pierre Le Barré continued, 'It is not the original, pretty crude I would say but it may get some shady people out of the woodwork, so to speak.' Junge looked around and said, 'I suggest we keep it strictly biological with no other hints or guesses, just like a fun thing among malacologists.'

At the neighbouring table was a couple enjoying their meal. The young lady had her back to the two academics and her companion was on the other side of the table facing her. The lady had a handbag next to her. Inside was a running tape recorder fed by a highly sensitive microphone only a short distance from Martin Junge and Pierre Le Barré. Her name was Danielle Laplace, the great-great-granddaughter of the famous mathematician and philosopher Pierre-Simone Laplace. Across from her was a French agent from Direction de La Surveillance du Territoire or DST. He was not her boyfriend. His name was Charles, a third-generation French Algerian.

10

The following morning, the delegates gathered in the lecture theatre at nine. They were all in a happy mood with high expectations of today's program. The chair of the morning was the Director of the laboratory, Dr Pierre Le Barré. Professor Junge, who had now recovered, was giving the day's introductory lecture: The History of Pearling.

Professor Junge slowly came to the podium but eventually got his papers in order and began his lecture: 'Humans have desired pearls for a long time through history. Most bivalves, freshwater or marine, produce pearls but the desired shape is a perfect sphere and the bigger, the more valuable it is. We know that the word "pearl" was written in Chinese about 1,000 BC but pearl-collection is much older. In Chinese waters, ancient fishers searched for molluscs for food and probably became the first pearl hunters to discover the value of the shine and lustrous lure of pearls. It was the Akoya pearls of the genus Pinctada. The Akoya pearls became sought after throughout the ancient world because of their beauty and shine. They were believed to be a gift from God or the tears of God. But it did not take long before other pearl oysters were exploited and fished for both food and pearls. Even up to modern times, pearl luggers operated along the Northern Western Australian coast.'

Professor Junge coughed and drank some water before he continued, 'In ancient times, pearls were associated with symbols of female purity and innocence. Pearls have been an element in a Hindus legend believed to be 5,500 years old and in a 4,000-year-old Chinese story. They are the symbol of wealth in the Hebrew and the Christian Bible. The Romans thought they were tears of the gods fixed in time inside of oysters. An anecdote claims that Cleopatra once bet Marc Anthony she would give the world's most exorbitant dinner party. To win the bet, she arrogantly crushed one of her pearl earrings and drank it in a goblet of wine. I do not know whether Mark Anthony had a taste of the wine but the one earring was said to be worth 100,000 pounds of silver. In any case, pearls have since ancient times also been used for medical purposes.'

Professor Junge took a deep breath and continued, 'Unfortunately, the desire for pearls have gone way beyond the exploration of pearl oysters. Today, we see largely uncontrolled destruction of mollusc populations searching for a simple blob of calcium carbonate and the fibrous protein conchiolin.' Professor Junge continued his historical account for another fifteen minutes until he looked out in the lecture theatre. He disappointingly observed a couple of listeners half-asleep with closed eyes. He raised his voice a bar and continued, 'I have never myself seen a pearl from a giant clam and certainly not from the largest one, Tridacna gigas. But in 1939, a Filipino American, Mr Wilburn Dowell Cobb, claimed to have bought a pearl of a giant clam from a fisherman in Palawan, a South Philippines province. The pearl weighed 14 pounds but is now locked up in a bank vault under a court's control because of a legal dispute. It is therefore not possible to confirm scientifically that it is a pearl of a giant clam.' Professor Junge looked at the audience and continued, 'Under all circumstances, pearls from cockles and most other bivalves other than pearl oysters are not likely to have the same lustre and spherical shape than those of the freshwater river mussels and saltwater pearl oysters of the genus Pinctada and none of them are known to produce a near perfectly round specimen.'

The professor looked at the chair and Pierre Le Barré was quick to say, 'Are there any questions? If not, I will then give the word to Mr Bruce Smith from Australia.'

Bruce, a powerfully built, sun-tainted man in his late fifties, entered the podium without any notes. He was wearing a suit that looked like an uncomfortable fit. His shoes were shiny and looked new. Initially, he had worn a tie but now his shirt was open three buttons down, exposing a red hairy chest.

Bruce started to speak straight away, 'G'day! As I understand it, this meeting is not about cultured pearls but giant clams. We have many giant clams along the reef but our only problem is to keep the slant-eyed Chinaman from taking them away.' Taken by surprise, Pierre Le Barré instantly looked up but did not intervene because the audience was just as surprised as the chair.

Bruce pushed on, 'What I am going to tell you today may be a surprise to some but it's on time to tell the truth.' Bruce looked at the audience as if he was ready to beat up a male crowd in a pub. He continued, 'For millennial, pearls have been admired by kings, queens and Daisy the cleaning lady down the street. The formation of pearls has been a mystery and subjected to all kinds of explanations from maladies to menaces. But the technique to produce pearly images of Buddha is Chinese. They introduced a jade figurine between the shell and the mantle allowing the figurine to be covered by acre. I travelled all the way to the Linnaean Society in London to examine the pearls believed to be developed by the Swedish naturalist Carl Linné somewhere in the 1770s but they were not perfect. Other people tried but failed. Then in 1906, two Japanese were hurrayed for discovering the secret of the pearl oyster. A patent application made up by each of the two characters ended up in court, resulting in a face-saving exercise where they agreed to joint ownership of the claim. I have spent years to find the truth about ownership of the culture technique and concluded that the technique was invented in Australia by William Saville-Kent in 1890. He established a pearl farm in Albany in 1906. I proved that the two Japanese gentlemen spent a lengthy time in Albany and met Mr Saville-Kent many times before they went home and filed an application. He even taught them to surf!'

Shouting, protests and profanities from the back of the room reached the podium and the chair got up to investigate. A couple of Japanese delegates were the cause of the noisy conundrum with raised arms and clenched fists. Pierre Le Barré commanded, 'Please, ladies and gentlemen, be quiet during the lecture!' Mr Bruce Smith pointed at the Japanese delegates and with a loud laugh shouted, 'Look at these slant-eyed donnybrooks. They are upset because I have revealed their lies!' Two angrily looking Japanese delegates were forcing their way up to the podium by pushing people away and reached Mr Bruce Smith screaming and shouting in their language. Both attempted a couple of punches but quickly realised that they had underestimated the size and athletic attire of Bruce Smith. He grabbed both combatants by the collarbone and pushed them away, much to the audience's amusement.

Pierre Le Barré shouted ineffectively from his chair and eventually directly into Mr Bruce Smith's ear, 'Will you please sit down!' He grabbed the microphone and shouted, 'Ladies and gentlemen. This behaviour is unacceptable. I will immediately terminate the meeting for a break until we have sorted things out.'

Things did not sort out. The two Japanese delegates and Mr Bruce Smith accepted their disagreement and looked at each other in disgust.

After an extended lunch, where Pierre La Barré tried to mediate between the two parties, the delegates were back in the auditorium for the final presentation. Rumours have already circulated that a research award was to be announced. Excitement filled the room when everybody had found their place. The afternoon chair was Professor Martin Junge and he took his time knowing and feeling the audience's attention. He enjoyed it when his audience was cooking in its fat; he uses to say jokingly to his colleagues. Some found it a bit arrogant but such behaviour was not unusual among senior academics. Eventually, he walked up on the podium and placed himself on a chair behind a small table. Reluctantly, he spoke into the microphone in front of him, 'Ladies and gentlemen! I will like to invite Captain Alex William Sidney

Smith to present his lecture on "The latest information on pearls from the giant clam, Tridacna gigas".'

Alex walked slowly to the podium with his notebook and looked firmly at the audience. It was clear to everybody that he was in control of his situation despite his relatively young age. The audience immediately turned quiet. He was well-dressed in civilian clothes and only his tie indicated that he was from the British navy. He began, 'Ladies and gentlemen! Today we are aware of two pearls believed to be from the giant clam, Tridacna gigas. Their rarity is not unusual considering its restricted distribution area which ranges from the Philippines to Northern Australia and from Fiji in the East to Sumatra in the West.'

A distribution map appeared on the screen and Alex continued, 'Tridacna gigas share this distribution area with the other species in this group of cockles but the second-largest species, as shown on the map, are distributed over a larger area than its cousin, from the centre of distribution to the African Coast, the Arabian peninsula and India and further east to Fiji. The second-largest clam is Tridacna maxima.'

Alex looked at the audience, whose eyes were focused on the distribution map. Satisfied, he continued, 'There are two pearls described in the popular literature which originated from the Palawan Sea in the South Philippines. They may very well be the same because the same person described them in the Natural History Magazine, published in the US by a Mr Wilburn Dowell Cobb in 1939. Considering that Mr Cobb provides two stories about the pearl years apart and provide its weight to be 6.4 kilograms and a maximum length of 24 centimetres and no further measurements, we can safely conclude that there is indeed one pearl only. His story is nevertheless entertaining but probably a curiosity from a scientific point of view.'

Alex looked in his notebook and said, 'Story number one: In 1934, Mr Cobb travelled in the Palawan area and discovered that a tribal chief had what he called a giant clam pearl to distinguish it from a gemstone pearl. The tribal chief considered it a sacred pearl because it resembled a turbaned head of a man whom he believed to be of the Islamic prophet, Muhammad. Mr Cobb offered to buy the pearl but it was refused. According to Mr Cobb, he saved the life of the chief's son, who suffered from malaria. In gratitude, the chief sold the pearl to Mr Cobb after he has named it "The Pearl of Allah".'

Alex looked at a copy of the Natural History Magazine and continued, 'Shortly after the publication, I travelled to the US to meet Mr Cobb in person and to study his pearl in detail. Mr Cobb did not provide further details other than what he wrote in the magazine but the pearl was what he had described. With a good imagination, one can recognise a turbaned head on one side of the pearl, which is irregular.'

Alex looked at the audience and felt that he had their attention and continued, 'Story number two: Then shortly before I was about to leave, Mr Cobb provided a different story about the pearl. In 1939, he had met a Chinese man, named Mr Lee, who claimed that the pearl was first grown in a smaller clam by inserting a small, flat jade figurine of a turbaned head of the founder of Taoism, Lao Tzu, deep between the mantle of the clam and the shell wall. The insertion, Mr Cobb claimed, was done more than 2,500 years ago by a disciple. During hundreds of years, Mr Cobb believed that the pearl had been transferred to ever greater-sized clams and finally reach the size and weight it has today. Mr Cobb believed that the pearl had ended up in Palawan due to wars and now called it "The Pearl of Lao Tzu". However, fancy this story might be, we know that the Chinese had for a long time mastered the technique of inserted a nucleus between the mantle and the shell, which results in it being coated by nacre. Therefore, I cannot dismiss Mr Cobb's story completely. However, Mr Cobb was unwilling to allow his pearl to be examined scientifically to establish its origin.'

After a short pause, Alex continued his lecture, 'A second pearl was once owned by Catherine the Great. It was named "The Sleeping Lion" due to its unusual shape. It weigh 114 grams and is 7 cm long. It is believed to have been formed in South-Eastern China between 1700 and 1760. The Sleeping Lion was purchased by Dutch merchants from Batavia who then brought it to Europe. In 1765, Hendrik Coenraad Sander, the accountant for the Dutch East India Company, became the first European owner of The Sleeping Lion. After his death, the pearl was acquired by Catherine the Great. The Empress of Russia kept the pearl in the Hermitage Museum in St Petersburg, where it was on public display until 1796. In 1865, a Dutch goldsmith purchased The Sleeping Lion and brought it to Amsterdam where it is today.'

Alex looked out at the lecture theatre and said, 'This ends my story but I have an announcement.' He looked at excited faces realising that rumours were already circulating.

He announced, 'The Royal Society of London and the French Académie des Sciences of Paris has decided to offer a sum of £25,000 to a person or persons who can scientifically prove or disprove the existence of pearls in or from the giant clam, Tridacna gigas. It is a pre-condition that the clam under no circumstances must suffer or die from such an investigation. Archaeological studies and material is accepted.' Instantly, loud applause broke out, followed by eager conversations between the delegates. Director Pierre Le Barré decided to stand up and calm the audience because the chairman, Professor Martin Junge, appeared deep into his thoughts. After a while, it was again silent. Alex continued, 'To claim the prize, participants have to register their biological interest and affiliation at the Royal Society of London within 14 days of today. Thank you so much.'

11

Alex left the podium and sat down on the seat he had left. Next to him to his right was Danielle Laplace. She had an open book in her lap. On the page was an image of a Scarlet Pimpernel, a simple flower with the Latin name, Anagallis arvensis and next to it three words in Latin: Dissimuluto, Deceptio, Exitum. Alex glanced without turning his head but then turned, looking directly in her eyes and said, 'I am sorry but I could not help myself. I see that you are interested in botany?' Danielle immediately closed the book and placed it in her bag.

With a conscientious face, she pensively answered, 'Yes, it is my occupation!' Hastily, Alex wrote something in his notebook and showed it to Danielle. It was a flower and three capital letters DDE, Disguise, Deception and Disappearance. He immediately closed his notebook, turned towards Danielle and said in a low voice. 'Would you like to join me for dinner?' Danielle nodded, got up and, followed by Alex, walked towards the exit.

After the meeting had ended, the delegates scattered all over the town for dinner. Pierre Le Barré and Professor Martin Junge met in the director's office to discuss the situation. Another guest was in the office. It was "Charles", the agent from Direction de La Surveillance du Territoire, or DST. It was the first time that he and Professor Junge were introduced to each other. It was late Friday and the discussions were brief. Professor Junge declared that he believed that Mr Bruce Smith and his two Japanese adversaries were heading to Australia and possible South-East Asia searching for pearls. My team and I will join them. By no means cooperatively or within sight but to do my studies there. He made sure that his intentions were loud and clear. Professor Junge did not want a French agent to follow him as a sniffer dog. He did not like his look and was unsure why he was in Le Barré's office. Professor Junge shook hands with the two men and within long he was on his way to catch a plane from Brest to London.

Alex and Danielle walked along the cobblestoned streets looking for a café or small restaurant with few or no delegates. Danielle suggested a place further out along the coast, which she knew well. They walked through the harbour, now dry at low tide with fishing boats standing on the bottom, each supported by a large pole secured to the hull by heavy iron brackets and leaning against the dock wall. Occasionally, Alex got ahead and turned around as if he was looking at Danielle but he was checking whether anyone followed. After half-an-hour walk, they arrived at a small tavern in a two-storey house. There were only a few guests, all Bretons. Conversation stopped as soon as the couple entered but quickly resumed after Danielle had asked in French, her native language, 'Good evening, any chance for a table and a meal?'

The proprietor jumped up and loudly exclaimed, '*Oui, Mademoiselle, oui!*' With a smile he put his right hand on her waist while gesturing with his left. Articulating in a fast flow of French the proprietor guided her towards a table isolated from the bar where most of the Bretons were.

Danielle and Alex sat down. She looked at Alex with a smile and said, 'The menu for tonight is a lobster-crab soup and steamed Sole. I think it will be all right, don't you think so?' Baguettes and cheese quickly arrived along with a bottle of crisp white wine. Danielle looked at Alex and said in a low voice, 'You chose not to mention the Pearl of Saint-Sulpice?'

'Yes,' he answered, 'I don't think there is any need to advertise broadly. If these clam-people know something, they will tell. The best approach will be to go through the statements of those who join the giant clam competition and then ask them about the pearl. After the deadline, I will provide a list of the submitted projects to all participants. I think it will be fun.'

Danielle nodded while taking a sip of her wine. 'Do you know the value of the pearl if found?' she asked.

'We reckon between one to two million US dollars,' Alex answered. 'The British or French government cannot claim ownership of the pearl because of its history. It's finders, keepers, I believe.'

'And losers, weepers—what about the Scarlet Pimpernel?' Danielle asked. Alex slowly scanned the room but there did not appear to be any listeners.

In a low voice, he said, 'When your great-great grandfather, Pierre-Simon, died in 1827, there was no need for the Scarlet Pimpernel anymore because the Bourbons were in power. My great-great grandfather lost faith in the Royal Navy and the family moved to France. He died in 1840. Sir Percy Blakeney visited the family in France many times but as I understand it, they just enjoyed talking about their achievements in the past.'

The soup arrived and their conversation took a temporary pause. The enjoyment was beyond Alex's expectation but not Danielle's; she expected that. She knew the proprietor and the chef, his wife, very well. Alex looked at Danielle with a confounding and somewhat mischievous smile. Her whole appearance and charming behaviour made him partly spellbound. He had to remind himself that he was on a mission.

'I was looking through Sir Williams many diaries and notes which he kept in meticulous order as a ship's logbook. In the family library, copies of the letters he had sent and letters he had received are there, as wells as all his records. It's a substantial volume and it seemed to me that nobody had given it much attention. Nevertheless, for an essay, an assignment when I was at the officer academy in the Royal Navy, I was interested in his records from the siege of Arce and in particular of Sir William's strategic decisions. I came across a report about an Ottoman diplomat, Solayman Hamadani. Sir William mentions that an embassy employee in Constantinobel had paid a visit to a diplomat imprisoned by the Ottoman ruler, Selim the third. It appears that Mr Hamadani was a so-called crypto-jew with a changed family name. Knowing that he possibly would be executed, he told the British diplomat that he, on order from Haim Farhi, Pasha Al-Jazzar's right-hand man, had removed the Pearl of Saint-Sulpice, bringing it to the Famagusta Synagogue for safe-keeping. His motivation for doing so is unclear but Sir William refers it to Zionism.'

Alex paused and sipped on his wine. Danielle listened with attention. Their plates were removed and replaced with two fresh ones with Sole in a lemon cream sauce. The arrival of food made a temporary pause in their conversations. But that did not deter Danielle, who with typical French elegance encouraged Alex to continue. 'Sir William had made a note that it was unfortunate that Mr Hamadani was imprisoned and that they should make all efforts to free him. I assume that he was a British spy.'

Danielle responded quickly, 'No, I believe that he was a French spy, leaning to the Royalist side.' She put her fork and knife down and looked at Alex and said, 'There was an exchange of encrypted messages between Sir William, Sir Percy and then Marquis Laplace if you absolutely have to use titles.' With difficulty, Alex absorbed the critique of his use of titles but sustained from any comments.

'You know, Alex, in France, we have been through many revolutions and the term Égalité is deeply rooted in our society!'

Danielle gave Alex a mischievous smile and said in an eager tone, 'Come on, come on, don't let that deter you!'

'Ok,' Alex said, 'so you think that the Scarlet Pimpernel plotted an attempt to free Mr Hamadani?'

Danielle gave a quick answer, 'Yes, I think they succeeded and furthermore, they planned to remove the Pearl of Saint-Sulpice from the Famagusta Synagogue as a part of the bargain. To satisfy the Zionist's they had to make it look like a Muslim operation to confuse Pasha Al-Jazzar, who was on their heels.' Danielle leaned back to watch Alex's reaction; it revealed little but in his eyes were a particular shine of admiration and she could feel it. Alex had a defeated feeling and asked, 'Well, that's interesting, so who do you think removed the Pearl of Saint-Sulpice from the Synagogue?'

The answer was quick, 'A secret society which has existed in many years, the Aphrodite Society of Cyprus. It has many prominent international members, particularly during the romantic period in the early 19th-century—they are all romantic fanatics.' With poorly concealed excitement, Danielle took a sip of her wine.

Feeling subdued, Alex leaned back in his chair and in a low voice said, 'It seems that we have revived the League of the Scarlet Pimpernel.' Danielle looked at Alex over her wine glass and nodded.

The proprietor removed their plates, looked mesmerised at the two and asked, 'Any dessert?' Danielle declined politely and Alex agreed. She ordered coffee and cognac without asking Alex but she knew that he would agree.

12

Dr Kamal Bashour did not waste any time in Roscoff and boarded a fast train to Paris, expecting to catch a plane to Monaco. He sat relaxed and looked out of the window allowing the endless fields of artichokes to pass. For minutes without end, the train drove in a ditch deeper than the carriage windows, irritatingly obscuring his view. Bashour thought about the meeting. He was surprised that Professor Junge had openly admitted he was wrong about the amoebocytes and had conceded that the clams actually had, in fact, ciliated channels allowing the symbionts to enter and leave. He thought about how he, as a young scientist, had to defend himself when dragged before the Dean of the Faculty because of an insulting letter from a British professor. The editor of the journal Nature was less critical because the second reviewer had accepted the micrographs, although with some reservation. He was asked to submit other micrographs and even fresh ones but in the end, his paper was accepted. It was a bitter-sweet victory.

There were always critical comments about his work. Eventually, he had to leave the university department for a minor position in the fisheries in Al-Gurdaqa, a small town on the coast of the Red Sea facing the tip of the Sinai Peninsula, the Ras Muhammed. There was a small marine laboratory and a library left behind by the British when they departed in 1949. He considered the library as a gift from heaven and did not waste his time. Over the years, he conducted several studies of the coral reefs of the Red Sea and published his results in international journals. His obligations to the fisheries did not take much of his time.

He gained a reputation as a specialist in the Red Sea reef systems. He was invited to participate in international cruises on well-equipped research vessels with his overseas colleagues. It was highlights of his career and now sitting on a fast train from Roscoff to Paris he thought about it. When they dived off Ras Muhammed, Bashour and his diving buddy, a French diver from the Oceanographic Institute in Monaco discovered a pile of giant clam shells which appeared to be deposited on deeper water off the reef edge. The depth limited coral growth, so the clams had little marine fouling. There were other items around and he got the impression that they might have come from a sunken ship. His diving buddy was less interested but Bashour wrote down his observation and their position. He checked with the captain of the vessel several times. Some years later, he received a letter from the Oceanographic Institution in Monaco, yet again inviting him on a cruise. His old diving buddy asked him whether he had the notes still on the pile of clam shells they found; the cruise objective was to explore several archaeological sites they previously had recorded.

Bashour sat at the window and across sat another man he did not know. It was Charles from DST. There were no other people in the compartment. Charles looked at Bashour and, in Arabic, said, 'Mr Bashour, I presume?'

Bashour looked up, taken by surprise and answered, 'Yes, I am Bashour.'

Charles looked him straight in the eyes and said, 'Have you heard about the Pearl of Allah?'

Reluctantly, Bashour answered. After all, he was suspicious of strangers in particular because he could recognise the Algerian dialect. 'Yes, I attended a lecture at Station Biologique de Roscoff, given by a Mr William Sidney Smith from Britain. He mentioned a pearl, believed to be from a giant clam, given that name by an American, Mr Cobb—why do you ask?'

Charles continued, 'Yes, he did mention it but that pearl is likely to be a forgery. I am thinking about the real Pearl of Allah, the one which has been given a fatwa—it is also called the Pearl of Saint-Sulpice.' When Charles mentioned the word fatwa, Bashour got worried.

He felt a threat was likely to come his way and quickly answered, 'How should I know?'

Charles looked stiffly at Bashour while he slowly slid his right hand to the left and under his jacket and said, 'I am sure you do. Just in case you get your hand on it, I will remind you that every faithful Muslim has to return it to a mosque or to Mecca without hesitation unless you want to lose your head!' Charles moved his jacket a bit, exposing a shoulder holster likely to contain a handgun. At that moment, the conductor appeared in the doorway and asked to see the tickets. Bashour got up, gave his ticket to the conductor and grabbed his small suitcase. As soon as the conductor returned his ticket, he apologised to the conductor, who allowed him to pass out of the compartment to the corridor.

Bashour walked quickly down the corridor; several carriages down, he found the dining carriage. There were many people but he spotted an empty seat at a table with an elderly lady across. Politely he asked whether the seat was occupied but the lady was pleased with the prospect of a companion. Bashour sat down; he was now among other people and ordered a cup of coffee. It did not take long before he spotted Charles working his way through the carriages. While he passed Bashour, he remarked in Arabic without looking down, 'Remember, just remember.'

'What did he say?' the lady asked. Bashour shook his head lightly and said, 'Oh, it's nothing; he just apologised.'

13

When Professor Martin Junge was back in his Plymouth office, he started to phone friends and acquaintances, many with high government administration jobs, inquiring about the mysterious pearl. He had read about the Pearl of Allah described by the American Mr Cobb but he had not realised that there was a second one and was puzzled why the French had involved one of their agents. After hours on the phone, Junge nearly gave up because nobody seemed to know anything about a pearl and most asked him why he was interested in an old pearl. He could not provide a satisfactory answer.

Professor Junge tried the last call. He called an old school mate from his time at Eton. He knew his friend has had a long career in the Royal Navy and was now working for the Admiralty in the Ripley Building in London. *He must know something about Alex William Sidney Smith's assignment with the Royal Society,* he thought loudly.

After a lengthy conversation on their successful mutual careers and exchange of pleasantries such as, 'Martin, you have to come and dine with me in the club. Only old warriors come there, you know and sometimes it would be nice to chat with someone from the outside.' Professor Junge agreed and they fixed a tentative date. He was careful not to raise the question straight away but postponed it until the dinner became a reality. To his surprise, it did not take long. He received a call from his friend's secretary, who had organised a dinner at the Naval Club, Hill Street, Mayfair.

The professor felt comfortable in the Naval Club's luxurious environment; it was a far cry from King's College, where he previously worked. He was wearing a traditional dinner suit that immediately classified him as a civilian among all the navy brass. But that did not bother Professor Junge.

After a drink at the bar, the two friends sat down for dinner in an exclusive corner of the dining hall, separated by carved wooden screens and pot plants in troughs. After dinner, the two friends leaned back, enjoying their expensive red wine. Professor Junge then asked, 'Have you heard about Captain Alex William Sidney Smith?'

The reply came quickly, 'Why do you ask?'

Professor Junge paused and then answered, 'Recently, I attended a meeting about giant clams at Station Biologique in Roscoff. He appeared out of nowhere representing the Royal Society offering a handsome reward for those able to discover whether these clams produce pearls. He mentioned a large pearl, 14 pounds, I believe, called The Pearl of Allah, belonging to an American, Mr Cobb. The pearl is apparently locked up in a bank vault somewhere in the US due to a financial dispute. But he suggested that this pearl is fake. I naturally called the Royal Society but they were firmly closed as oysters at low tide. I wonder what it's all about.'

Junge's friend leaned back in his chair, took a sip of his red and said, 'The only thing I can tell you is that, Alex, whom I know very well, currently has an assignment with MI5. I cannot discuss his work; I am sure you will understand.'

'Of course,' Junge said. 'I did not expect you to reveal Navy secrets; yes, I do understand.'

'But, talking about pearls,' his Eton friend continued, 'I have heard an old story about a pearl, a large pearl brought to Britain during the French revolution by Antoine de Phélippeaux. He was one of Napoleon's main adversaries and a very competent artillery officer. Furthermore, he was one of the Scarlet Pimpernels and was instrumental in getting, who else but Sir William Sidney Smith out of the notorious Temple Prison. Antoine served for nearly four years in Armée de Condé in Germany and Switzerland and became one of our most trusted agents. He lost his life at the battle of Acre, where he fought on our side against Napoleon. He was a close friend of Sir William Sidney Smith and it was he who brought Antoine to Acre. I believe he brought the pearl with him.'

Professor Junge was silent and overwhelmed by the surprise. A sip of red wine brought him out of his thoughts. 'Do you by any chance know what the pearl was called?' Professor Junge tried.

'No,' his friend replied, 'I am sorry, old chap; that's the information I got.'

Professor Junge travelled back to Plymouth. His Eton friend and naval officer informed MI5 that Professor Martin Junge from the Plymouth Marine Laboratory had requested information about Captain Alex William Sidney Smith's activities. The report was quickly passed on to Alex at his routine briefing.

Back in his office, Professor Junge was thinking. *If he could find this pearl, he would become famous. Somehow, he believed that the pearl should be his because he was the only British expert in giant clams and other cockles. 'I have devoted my life to the study of molluscs, he reasoned with himself, so who else could claim expertise in the subject?' Of course,* he thought, *it would be nice to receive the award of £25,000 from the Royal Society, not to mention the value of the pearl but the award would come nicely to support his meagre university pension. It was not the prospective earnings that drove him; it was academic prestige that was the most important. He didn't realise that he had, like many before him, become obsessed with the pearl.*

He did what a professor would do; initiated an extensive study. He wrote the essential question in his notebook, 'Where did the pearl go after the battle of Acre? 'He traversed available archives of naval activities, scanned through reports of who came and went, what provisions were brought aboard and whom and what left the HMS Tigre, Commodore Sir William Sidney Smith's battleship. It was then he came across the communications from the Commodore to the Admiralty that mentioned the imprisonment of the diplomat and British spy, Solayman Hamadani and along with it the mentioning of the recovery of a French pearl, as a matter of honour, carried out by the Scarlet Pimpernel. The professor could not find any further information. Professor Junge did not know what the Scarlet Pimpernel was, except that it was a fictive spy story from the French Revolution, which had previously been popular in theatres, movies and TV. He thought it was a joke and remembered that his Eton friend had mentioned the Scarlet Pimpernel, being a secret club of some kind. He could not believe that it was real.

After having spent many restless nights, allowing his obsession to grow and grow, Professor Junge decided to do it his way—independently. In all his research, he had kept everything for himself until his great moment when he would reveal it all to the astonishment and envy of his colleagues. He had always enjoyed that. He had only experienced one defeat and it was a constant irritant; his lost a scientific argument to an Egyptian. It was the lowest point in his career. His opponents in the science community had found prodigious pleasure in his defeat, fuelled by his arrogant behaviour and insatiable desire to be first. Professor Junge had never shown any sympathy for the less fortunate ones who just moved aside to avoid a conflict or an argument. He had to go back to Station Biologique in Roscoff, talk to his friend Director Pierre Le Barré and "Charles", the French agent from DST. Professor Junge wrote in his notebook: What do they know?

Captain Alex William Sidney Smith was busy preparing himself for an extended assignment in Cyprus. He was looking forward to meet Danielle Laplace again. He was hoping that she had made progress or had fresh ideas of where the pearl might be. *It may not be in Cyprus at all,* he thought, worrying him a bit. He knew that Danielle was working for UNESCO, preparing reports on the classification of the Aphrodite historical sites in Cyprus because the now independent country wanted them to be World Heritage Sites. She had told him that there was quite a bit of botany in it but he did not understand why. *Nevertheless,* he thought, *it is going to be fun.*

Alex had taken Professor Junge's enquiries seriously but they worried him. Alex had enquired about the French agent "Charles" and whether Danielle had any affiliation to the French secret service. Even if she had, he was sure that the French would not tell him. When they discussed "Charles", Danielle had said to him that Charles had asked her whether he could join her at the table when she was waiting in the basement restaurant opposite the laboratory. She could hardly refuse because the restaurant was so crowded. She was embarrassed over Alex's question as if she was interrogated and had told him that it was none his business. He quickly apologised and she noted a flush on his face. She decided not to say to him that she had listened to the conversations at the table behind.

Alex had organised two of his people to shadow Professor Junge. His office at MI5 would study his past. They did not find anything interesting or relevant for the case but kept up their surveillance. Soon they learned that Professor Junge had booked a ticket to the ferry from Plymouth to Roscoff, a six-hour day trip. Alex decided to send his agents along with Professor Junge on the ferry with the instruction to listen to Pierre Le Barr'és office. They pretended to be marine biologists and had applied for laboratory space at the station a few days in advance. Soon, Alex received a phone call from the agent in charge, explaining that the harbour and the laboratory were swarming with what he believed to be French agents. The French agents had been awaiting Professor

Junge's arrival and monitored his every step from the ferry to the laboratory. But there was no sign of Charles anywhere.

14

Alex decided to go to Roscoff immediately and booked a small plane to fly him across the channel. His secretary had found accommodation for him in a cottage on the coast, just outside Roscoff. He changed his appearance lightly with large spectacles, a tweed jacket and a checkered shirt with a bow tie, commonly worn by British academics. As soon as he arrived at Station Biologique, he walked upstairs to the library where the communist librarian was at her usual desk, despatching a hostile look over her glasses at any intruder. Alex requested two books on molluscs in fluent French making the librarian a little more cooperative. 'Anglaise?' she asked.

'Oui,' Alex responded, already deeply into his book. He roughly knew where the Director's office was below and he had to find an excuse to be right over it. The library was quiet; nobody else was there. He could hear conversations below through the old floor planks, covered by linoleum sheets that had cracked with missing pieces everywhere.

Alex asked the librarian where the conversations came from and she threw out her right arm and said, 'It's the Director's office—they never shut up!' Then he got his chance when the librarian got up and walked out of the door, presumably for a toilet visit. Alex immediately found a place under a bookshelf where to place a sensitive microphone and a miniature tape recorder. He was back in his chair before the librarian returned. After a while, he left the library and walked back to his cottage.

When he arrived, he found one of his agents at the cottage. 'Charles has arrived,' he said. 'He has a meeting the same time as Professor Junge at ten in the morning. I believe that Mr Junge and Charles are dining out tonight.' In his agent's company, Alex prepared himself for the task and disguised himself as a Paris tourist having his meal at the local restaurant opposite the laboratory. He could not have his agents there because they looked out of place. He ordered them to return to London. Alex did not want any conflict with the French secret services.

Surely enough at about eight, Professor Junge arrived in the restaurant and seated himself in the little room where the customers had to wait over a drink if the restaurant was full. Alex was there too, pretending to be waiting for someone. Shortly after Charles arrived, he and Junge proceeded to the restaurant room. Alex stayed for a while before getting across the room to a table next to the two. Despite efforts to listen to the conversation, he could only obtain a scanty idea of what they were talking about. It appeared to be trivialities as if they both wanted to be better acquainted. It occurred to Alex that Charles might not be a French secret agent unless his gut feeling betrayed him. His suspicion was soon to be confirmed. When Alex returned to London with his tape recorder and sensitive microphone, his staff had gained information about Charles. It turned out that he was a French Algerian. Charles has had a past participating in the revolt against French rule being a part of an underground organisation called Organisation Armée Secrète or the OAS, mainly consisting of French military personnel. The OAS wanted Algeria to remain French and carried out many bombings and murders both in Algeria and in France to stop the planned independence. Charles was currently working for an American company specialising in the recovery of lost or stolen art.

Alex carefully listened to the tapes from the library. He could only get bits of the information because every time the librarian walked over the floor, it sounded as a herd of elephants passing. The work and skills of a sound technician almost revealed the full conversation. The meeting in Pierre La Barrè's office had developed into an interrogation of the professor. It appeared as Pierre and Charles have some association but the tape did not clarify that association's nature. The interrogation was about the Pearl of Allah. It was clear that Charles was looking for the pearl on behalf of an undisclosed organisation. After a while, the conversation stopped to the sound of coffee cups being distributed. Then, to Alex's surprise, he heard Charles offering Professor Jung a substantial sum of money if he could find the Pearl of Saint-Sulpice, alias the Pearl of Allah.

15

Charles had spent his adult life in wars. He had never seen anything else until the end of the Algerian War. His parents were indigenous Muslim Algerians. His father had served in the French army as an officer. When the Algerian conflict broke out in 1954, Charles was sixteen years old. His father was instrumental in organising the so-called Harkis, a military pro-France army numbering about 200,000 soldiers, fighting the Front de Libération Nationale, the FLN. The FLN had taken up arms against France in Algiers, demanding independence. Charles joined the Harkis. He was trained in guerrilla warfare, carried out assassinations and all kinds of covert operations, usually with a deadly result. The Algerian war was brutal.

In 1962, the conflict ended and Charles and his family were forced to flee to France. In Algeria, the Harkis were seen as traitors and those who stayed behind suffered reprisals by FLN or lynch mobs. In France, life was not easy for the Harkis but his father's rank and importance helped the family. Through his father's connections, Charles got a training appointment in le Direction de le Surveillance du Territoire or DST, the French counter-espionage organisation. The DST quickly recognised his talent and experience and soon he was appreciated as a valuable asset. Charles, however, as an indigenous Algerian Muslim had never accepted his fate but returning to Algiers when the FLN was in power was not an option. When assigned to a job in Marseille, he could not resist the call for the Friday prayers in a local mosque. A man approached him, introducing himself as Egyptian. His name was Amun Hassan. After the prayer, they met in a small café close to the mosque. Charles was surprised to see many Harkis and he recognised a few as former brothers in arms. Amun talked about an Arabic Muslim organisation dissatisfied with North Africa and Palestine's current political situation, fighting for a larger Pan-Arabian State. He argued for a holistic view of statehood and regarded all the current Arabic states to be nothing more than a colonial by-product. After all, they all believe in Islam and the virtue of Islamic Laws. Charles agreed to support Amun Hassan if he could and they exchanged details for communication.

After a while, Charles realised that his association with Amun might jeopardise his engagement with DST. They discussed this and within long Amun offered Charles a job in an American Company, which retrieved stolen or lost antiquities, the Mesopotamian or MESO. Charles learned that it was a well-funded American-Arabic company set up to recover Islamic art stolen by the western colonial powers. But that was a facade. The company carried out covert operations all over the Middle-East to promote Islamic policies. In Annapolis, Maryland, in the MESO headquarters, Charles was introduced to the Pearl of Allah as his first assignment.

16

On the dusty road between Paphos and Polis in Cyprus, Danielle was driving a white Jeep with UN markings. It was spring; the time when the Troodos Mountains were in flower. Danielle had visited many sites looking for orchids. She was particularly interested in those associated with the Aphrodite cult but as a botanist her interests were much broader. The UNESCO assignment was to collect data and to write reports allowing the Aphrodite cult's archaeological sites to be added to the World Heritage List. She would not allow the opportunity to slip away, so she had established cooperation with botanists in Kew Botanical Gardens in Great Britain who worked on a book titled *Flora of Cyprus*. For now, she sampled plants for a herbarium in the Agricultural Research Institute in Cyprus. In every study of the distribution and abundance of vascular plants, a herbarium is essential because species must be correctly identified.

When she arrived in Polis, a small seaside town on the northwest of Cyprus, she stopped briefly for a traditional Greek black coffee. The proprietor, a traditionally dressed Greek Cypriot, greeted her with a warm smile shouting, 'Kalosórises sto Polis, neari kyría—welcome to Polis, young lady.' The café owner offered her honey-infused green walnuts with her coffee, something Danielle had never tasted before. She could not resist the offer which seemed to please the café owner. He asked her where she was heading because not many visitors were coming to Polis and rarely a single lady in a UN vehicle. Danielle explained that she was going to Aphrodite's bath to examine the flora in the spring's surroundings. That immediately attracted the interest of a couple of locals who were in the café drinking Ouzo. It did not last long before she had a full explanation of how to get to the bath and a complete historical chronicle. Danielle felt the typical hospitality and generosity of the Greek Cypriots. She remembered reading in a Cypriot in-flight magazine;

Be friendly with the peasantry, you will hear them tell interesting stories of village characters, their saints, quacks and wedding ceremonies.

Everybody in the café, including the owner's wife, who had emerged from the kitchen, waved Danielle goodbye, expecting her back for lunch.

Danielle had no problem finding the Chrysochous Valley entrance because there was a sign with the text 'Fontana Amorosa' and a large white arrow. She knew that the spring, Aphrodite's bath, was located where the valley meets the Akamas Peninsula's steep rocks, not far from the sea. Danielle parked the jeep and walked along a narrow path towards the rock wall. When she reached the end, she was amazed by the beauty of the place. Water was welling up from the rocks like soft rain, pouring into a small pond and further to the sea. The water looked inviting. She let her hand through the water, which was crystal clear and cool. Danielle was mesmerised by the lush and thick vegetation shading both the spring and the pond. She saw many trees which must have been around for quite a while like ficus, oak, thymus and many others. There were flowers everywhere. Danielle spotted cyclamen, gladiolus, anemone and cistus and was overwhelmed by their abundance. What attracted her attention was the abundance of orchids. She realised that there was a lot to do. Danielle stood up, let her hand through her hair and loudly exclaimed, 'Now I understand; this must be the favourite place for the goddess of beauty.'

Danielle dropped her sampling gear and botanical press on a dry, vegetation-free, flat rock and walked around the pond. She made notes and noticed that the pond, surrounded by limestone rocks, was not deep. She followed the narrow groove with dense vegetation towards the sea but it was blocked and she could not go any further. Then she found a passage to the left through thick bushes and was surprised to find a large area with water-soaked mosses. Among the mosses, flat limestone rocks were everywhere, all with numerous, larger soil-filled crevices with orchids. For Danielle, it was sensational, a Paradise for botanists.

She decided to start at the spring and quickly found three orchid species. There was one she expected to find; it was Serapias aphrodite, Aphrodite's orchid. There were two other species, which she identified after consulting her flora. They were Orchis italica and Orchis simia. She knew that Aphrodite's orchid, which grows at Aphrodite's bath, is only found there and nowhere else. The two other species can be found in many places in Cyprus and around the Mediterranean. There were butterflies everywhere, especially a blue one.

Danielle decided to skip lunch and work through the day. Before she left Polis, she had booked a room in a small hotel. She was happy with that decision because her assessment would likely take some time.

Danielle worked methodologically through the orchids among the mosses and concentrated on the various springs and ponds along the Akamas rock face. To her surprise, she found another passage through fallen rocks leading her further away from Aphrodite's bath and into a gulley. An area opened up in front of her, a similar open space of flat limestone perforated by numerous crevices with seeping groundwater like the ones she had seen before. Mosses were growing everywhere and in patches of soil many orchids. But what caught her eye was a pond, slightly smaller than the one at Aphrodite's Bath further out of the valley. It appeared to be deep; she could not see the bottom but she could recognise the depth when she wore her sunglasses. Danielle made notes and drew sketches before returning to her primary task, describing the flora at the Baths of Aphrodite.

By the end of her day, she had an extensive collection of the vascular plants growing in the cryptic environment on the lower plateau next to the Akamas rock face. Everything she collected was kept moist in plastic bags, which she brought back to her hotel room for further processing and pressing.

At early dusk, she arrived at the small cobble-stoned square in the middle of Polis; the group of elderly Greek men with their worry beads and a glasses of Ouzo were still there. The men carefully watched her while having a quiet conversation.

Danielle parked the jeep and started to carry her equipment and samples up to her room. Immediately one of the men in the café called out loudly, 'Dimitrios!' A young man appeared from the kitchen. The man who called pointed towards Danielle and Dimitrios ran across the square, grabbed one of Danielle's boxes and continued up the stairs to her room. Danielle ensured Dimitrios that she did not need his help but he continued helping her until all her boxes were in her room. Danielle tried to give him a tip but he refused and disappeared back to his pots and pans in the kitchen. Eventually, she could sit down on the bed. She was exhausted. She decided to wait until the morning before finishing the samples.

Danielle's room had a spacious balcony and as darkness fell she opened the French doors; she realised that her room had a magnificent view over the bay. Now, all the lights had come on in the village. Out of nearly every building and courtyard came the smell of food prepared on charcoal mixed with low voices and laughter. She could hear the sounds of animals from all the farms in the hills and valleys. The smells and the sounds amazed her and gave her an exhilarating feeling. She thought about rainy London and how lucky she was to be here in Cyprus's mild spring, Aphrodites Cyprus. She decided to change her field clothing, refresh herself and go down to the café for dinner.

When she approached the café across from her hotel, the owner's head popped up and he shouted, 'Kalosórises, nears kyría—welcome, young lady!' He guided her to a table under his vines and clapped his hand three times. Dimitrios's head popped out of the kitchen and he arrived at the table with a carafe of cold water and a glass. Behind Dimitrios the owner's wife looked out to see what all the fuss was about but quickly returned to the kitchen. Danielle asked for a small carafe of his best red wine, which his son Dimitrios promptly delivered. The owner then looked at Danielle while pointing at his chest and said, 'Alexios and my wife is Antonia; she is my flower; I love her so much!' His wife's face appeared in the kitchen doorway and gave Alexios an angry look but he just waved back at her.

The mellow Cyprus wine went straight to Danielle's head, although she only had one sip. She decided to drink some water, something she had neglected during the day. An enjoyable meze appeared on her table and thereafter dishes of grilled lamb, vegetables and a salad. When Danielle had finished her meal, she recognised how hungry she had been and regretted skipping her lunch. She decided that at breakfast, she would ask Alexios for sandwiches to bring along.

Danielle realised that the small carafe of wine quickly disappeared but she asked Alexios for a Greek coffee. When the coffee appeared, it was accompanied by a small glass; Danielle recognised it as brandy. Alexios smiled and said, 'It's on the house.' She sat back and relaxed watching families with children enjoying Antonia's and Alexios' great food. From the café, the sounds of an Accordion accompanied by a Bouzouki filled the air, supported by spontaneous singing. Danielle thought that the songs sounded melancholic but soon she picked up the refrains and joined in quietly while warming her brandy.

Next to Danielle's table sat an elderly man counting his worry beads while joining the singing in a low voice. After a while, he politely asked Danielle whether she had visited Aphrodite's Bath. 'Yes,' she said, 'I have been there all day.' The man nodded with a smile and said, 'Beautiful and mysterious, don't you think?' She nodded. He continued, 'Here we all know Aphrodite; she is one of us. She is a beautiful woman but beware she is also a warrior.' He had a smile all over his face. Danielle thought she should ask only to test. 'Does Aphrodite loves pearls?'

To Danielle's surprise, the man got up, jumped up on his chair and looked towards the musicians who stopped playing. He then looked over the heads of all the café guests and, in a serious voice of citation, loudly exclaimed;

Often she guided the straying clusters of floating hair and arranged them even rows down to her forehead; she touched up the plaits with sweet-scented oil—stir it and the far spreading scent of the unguent intoxicates heaven, the sea and the whole earth. She put on her head a coronet of curious work, set with many rubies, the servant of love; when they move, the Cyprian flame sends out bright sparkling.

The orator paused for a few seconds and then continued in a more emphasising tone while looking at Danielle.

She also wore that stone which draws man to desire, which has the bright name of the desire-stuck Moon and the stone which is enamoured of iron the love producing and the Indian stone of love, offspring itself of the waters akin to the Foam-born and the blue sapphire still beloved of Phoibos.

Following the applause, he gestured swinging his arm, bowed and jumped down from the chair.

'That was amazing,' Danielle softly exclaimed while clapping her hands a few times. 'As I understand you, the

Indian stone of love must be a pearl because you said it comes from the water akin to the foam-born and that must be Aphrodite.'

The elderly man smiled with an understanding look as if he was listening to a child and said, 'Yes, you are a sharp listener. You are right. It's a passage from our beloved Nonnus Dionysiaca, an ancient Greek epic poem.'

Slowly, the music and singing started, giving Danielle a feeling of mild melancholy. The elderly man next to her quietly sang along. He turned towards Danielle and said, 'This song is called *Athenian Girl*. It's a sad love song like so many of our old songs.' He hummed the tune and waited until the music stopped, then he sang in English;

I stay awake in Athens because of you, my little one.
And every day because of you, I find my devil.
Because of you, I drink wine; because of you, I get drunk.
If you want Athenian girl to live with me, then the fire you lit inside, be sure to extinguish it, don't play your tricks with me, you got involved with me—you can't just get rid of me.

Someone shouted,' Evagoras, Evagoras,' and with his hand indicated that he wanted the old man to stand up, which he slowly did. A colourful discussion and articulation across the room followed. Evagoras got up on his chair and exclaimed while opening his arms, 'This one is Homer's Hymn to Aphrodite.'

Muse, tell me the things done by golden Aphrodite, the one from Cyprus, who arouses sweet desire for gods and who subdues the races of mortal humans and birds as well, who fly in the sky, as well as all beasts—all those that grow on both dry land and the sea.

They all know the things done by the one with the beautiful garlands, the one from Kythera.

But there are three whose minds she cannot win over or deceive.

The first is the daughter of aegis-bearing Zeus, bright-eyed Athena.

For she takes no pleasure in the things done by golden Aphrodite.

What does please her in wars and what is done by Ares, battles and fighting and the preparation of splendid pieces of craftsmanship?

For she was the first to teach mortal humans to be craftsmen in making war-chariots and other things on wheels, decorated with bronze.

And she it is who teaches maidens, tender of skin, inside the palaces, the skill of making splendid pieces of craftsmanship, putting it firmly into each one's mind.

Evagoras stopped, jumped down from his chair while the audience applauded. Danielle saw sweat running down his forehead and neck. With a bright red handkerchief, he dried his face and with a deep breath sank a bit into his chair. 'I think I am getting too old for this,' he said with a smile.

Danielle smiled and quietly clapped her hands. 'This was an excellent performance and thank you for using an English translation,' she said, padding him on his arm.

The following day Danielle was up early, brought her camera equipment down to her jeep and drove away after she had collected her sandwiches. With sleepy eyes, Alexios gave them to her in the doorway of the café kitchen. She jumped into the jeep and drove off to Fontana Amorosa. At the spring, Danielle worked all morning, taking photographs of all plants and the surroundings from various angles. She was happy with the morning light and the crisp air which increased the contrast and the colours. Danielle concentrated on reducing shadow effects by using several small flashes. At noon, she stopped, having exposed more than 15 roles of colour slides. Danielle packed her cameras and photographic gear into their respective transport boxes and carried them out one by one to her jeep. During the day, Danielle looked many times up towards the Akamas plateau above. She had a feeling that she was being watched but did not see anything that could back up her suspicion; she rejected the thought. If Danielle had asked someone in Polis, her suspicion would have been confirmed but any fear would have been calmly dismissed with the words, 'Aphrodite's bath is mysterious but beautiful women will always be protected.'

Danielle drove straight down to Polis and her hotel to pack her belongings in the jeep and pay her bill. As she was getting into the jeep, Alexios came running from his café waving his right arm shouting, 'Don't leave, don't leave!' He held up a bottle of red wine and handed it to her. 'It's a small goodbye gift, just for you.' Danielle smiled and accepted the bottle, which had a blue label with a figure of Aphrodite with the text: Aphrodites Claret. She thanked Alexios many times and ensured him that she would return.

17

Kamal Bashour had been two weeks on-board the research vessel Calypso from the Oceanographic Institute of Monaco. The ship had visited sites of archaeological interest along the northern reefs of the Red Sea. Eventually, they arrived at the site Kamal previous had found. At the bottom, next to a drop-off from the coral reef, he and his diving buddy had discovered many shells of giant clams. He assumed that the shells were old. They had no coral growth because, at that depth light levels are much less than above. On this cruise, he had more time to investigate the shells. He recovered a few, so that he could do a closer examination on-board. There were no artefacts among the shells that could indicate a wreck. On-board, he realised that the shells were not Tridacna gigas, the largest of the giant clams, which do not occur naturally in the Red Sea. It was the shells of Tridacna maxima, the second largest species which can be found in the Red Sea. He concluded that fishers had dumped the shells after having removed the meat. Kamal collected a couple of shells for age determination. He decided that spending more time on Calypso was a waste of time and returned to his laboratory in Al-Gurdaqa on the Egyptian side.

As soon as Kamal arrived at the laboratory, he drilled out a series of samples from the shells and sent them to Cairo for age determination. He was convinced that the shells were not old but he owed the scientists in Monaco the final proof. Kamal packed a small suitcase and left for Alexandria. He wanted to visit the old library there and check the facts about the Pearl of Allah and if needed, order the documentations for the fatwa from the library in Mecca.

Within a week, Kamal had exhausted the library information available. He located a copy of the original fatwa. He found that it was issued due to the Portuguese attack on Muscat in 1507 rather than a dispute of ownership. The document stated that the pearl was brought to Muscat by Radhanite traders who had bought it in Maluku, the islands of sandalwood, cloves and nutmeg. They had offered the pearl for sale with the name "The Pearl of Allah". That upset several people of the Azdi Nabahinah clan who ruled Muscat at that time. Consequently, they seized the pearl, awaiting the return of the Imam of Muscat, who was to determine whether the pearl showed a true image of Allah.

With the assistance of the Imam of the Abu al-Abbas Al-Mursi Mosque in Alexandria, Kamal submitted a request to Mecca for information regarding the fatwa for the Pearl of Allah. After two weeks, documents arrived. The older documents dealt with the Pearl of Allah's appearance at the battle of Acre and the inquiry established by Pasha Al-Jazzar. In these documents, Kamal found a note suggesting that the pearl was probably in the hands of the British and that the pearl was taken by an unknown society in Cyprus, involving Haim Farhi, Pasha Al-Jazzar's Jewish adviser. The note was written in the Arabic language of Shia Law lawyers, the

Imams. Kamal consulted the Imam of the Alexandria mosque, who translated the text for him. The Imam asked Kamal why he was interested in this particular fatwa? He answered that it was of curiosity related to his interest as a marine scientist in giant clams. He explained that the Royal Societies in London and Paris had decided to offer a large sum of money to a person or persons, who could scientifically prove or disprove the existence of pearls in or from the giant clam, Tridacna gigas. The Imam looked worried and said, 'I have had an enquiry recently on this subject. It was an Algerian. He turned up unexpected at my office. I did not tell him more than what was in the documents from the library.' Kamal thanked the Imam for the information and told him that he had been threatened by a French-Algerian man on the train when he left Roscoff. The Imam looked worried and said, 'You better watch out. Old fatwa's can quickly evolve into dangerous situations. I will appreciate it if you keep me informed.' Kamal promised to do so and learned that the British had requested the Omani Sultan, Said Ibn Taimur, to use his influence to withdraw the fatwa but that had not happened. The Imam returned a note to Mecca for the records. The Imam didn't know that another party had requested information from Mecca regarding the Pearl of Allah. It was the Directorate of Religious Affairs in Ankara under the direction of the Turkish government.

Kamal walked back from the Mosque along El-Gaish Road and the promenade along the coast towards the library. He needed to think about what he would do. He stayed at a small modest hotel in one of the side streets of El-Gaish.

In Monaco, Professor Martin Junge had waited for more than a week for the arrival of Calypso, the research vessel of the Oceanographic Institute of Monaco. He had exhausted all his sources, friends and acquaintances for information about the French pearl and was frustrated. He had tried to contact Alex William Sidney Smith but with no luck. His calls were met with, 'Sorry, sir, Captain Sidney Smith is not available.' Again, he tried the Royal Society but only got the wrath of an angry secretary who told him that they had no further information.

Professor Junge decided to swallow his pride and embarrassment. He was going to contact Dr Bashour and organise a meeting. To call the laboratory in Al-Gurdaqa in Egypt was a challenge because Junge did not speak Arabic and the people in the office did not speak English. The line was cut many times and he was on the brink of giving up. Then a final try gave a result. The operator said, 'Calypso—at sea.' Junge knew that the Calypso was a famous research vessel. In a call to Monaco, the laboratory secretary informed him that the ship was presently off Ras Muhammad on the Sinai Peninsula's tip, expected back in Monaco next week. They confirmed that Dr Kamal Bashour was onboard. Professor Junge packed his suitcase and caught a plane to Monaco with the expectation of meeting Dr Bashour when Calypso arrived. During a week, where Junge had felt the pain of the high hotel prices and had for hours restlessly walked up and down the waterfront of Port de Fontvieille waiting for Calypso which was behind schedule. When Calypso arrived, Junge quickly learned that Dr Bashour had disembarked at Ras Muhammad. Reluctantly, Professor Junge caught a plane to Cairo, spent a night at an expensive hotel at the airport before taking a smaller passenger prop to Al-Gurdaqa on the coast of the Red Sea. There was not much there—not a tree.

The only vegetation he saw from the air was a green patch at a small hotel. A taxi brought him there. The hotel was fine but the vegetation was a green plastic lawn.

The next day Junge made enquiries about the fisheries laboratory. He found out that it was situated 10 km north of the town. After arriving by bus, the only means of transport disregarding donkeys, Professor Junge stood in front of an office door with only a reminiscence of paint. He recognised that not just the door but the entire laboratory was in urgent need of a coat of paint. An office clerk in a traditionally long white Thobe and a Kufi skull cap knocked on Bashour's office door, ensuring that Professor Junge kept his distance. A voice answered, 'Udkhul—Come in.' The office clerk opened the door and, with a hand gesture invited Professor Junge to enter. With a surprised look on his face, Dr Bashour jumped up from his seat, walked straight over to Junge and grabbed his hand.

'Welcome, welcome—what a surprise; sit down, sit down!'

Kamal said something to the office clerk and when both men sat down, the clerk arrived with two glasses and a teapot with mint tea. The office clerk demonstrated his tea-mixing skills, which Kamal patiently waited for to be finished. When the clerk left the office, Kamal turned towards Junge and offered him the tea with a hand gesture. 'What a surprise,' Kamal said. 'I can't remember seen any British here since they left in 1947!'

Junge provided a forced smile and said somewhat embarrassed, 'But we left the whole coral reef marine library from the British Museum.'

'Yes, yes, you did and we are grateful for that. Now, what can I do for you?' Kamal asked.

Professor Junge took a sip of his tea and slowly said, 'I'm sorry for barging in unannounced—please, accept my apology.' Kamal nodded and Junge continued, 'Things have become strange after our meeting in Roscoff. What I thought should be interesting research and field investigation of pearls of the giant clams has turned out to be something entirely different.'

Junge looked at Kamal with a serious expression and suddenly said, 'Please, call me Martin. I will be pleased if you will use my first name.'

'Kamal is my name,' Kamal said and shook Junge's hand. Martin felt relieved and decided to tell Kamal everything he knew from his own perspective. He described the meeting in Pierre Le Barré's office where the French agent "Charles" appeared out of nowhere. He explained that Charles had introduced himself as an American company agent, specialising in the recovery of lost or stolen art and artefacts.

'In a very unpleasant way, he insinuated that I had special knowledge of a pearl he called the Pearl of Saint-Sulpice.' After a pause, Martin continued, 'When he realised that I did not know anything about it, his attitude changed completely and he offered me a large sum of money if I could find it and hand it over to him.'

'I have met this guy,' Kamal said. 'He threatened me on the train to Paris. He mentioned the Pearl of Saint-Sulpice, alias the Pearl of Allah and raved that every faithful Muslim was obliged to return it to a mosque or to Mecca without hesitation, unless one wants to lose the head. He said that the pearl in the US called "The Pearl of Allah" is fake.' With a smile, Kamal leaned back in his chair and folded his hands on his stomach.

'I have a proposal,' Martin said. 'An old schoolmate, working in the Admiralty in London, has told me that such a pearl is likely to exist. He suggested that it might be in Cyprus, where it is being kept by a society once supported by a network of secret agents called The Scarlet Pimpernel. What if we joined forces and travelled to Cyprus? Incidentally, there may be a shell of a giant clam found on a wine ship currently excavated off Kyrenia's harbour on the North coast of Cyprus. I have met the excavation leader, a young American, and he invited me to come over and check what they have.' Kamal was dumbfounded; Martin's proposal was a genuine surprise. On the one hand, he was wary of being too close to Professor Junge and his arrogant behaviours. Still, on the other hand, his proposal was appealing, an adventure, something different from his life in Al-Gurdaqa.

Kamal rang a bell and the office clerk appeared in the doorway. He ordered more tea which soon arrived. The lengthy pause kept Martin in nervous suspense. He wondered whether he had played all his cards too soon. When Kamal and Martin had sipped their tea, Kamal looked out of the window over the laboratory garbage dump full of goats and towards the sea. With a sigh, he turned towards Martin and said, 'It all sounds nice and possibly exciting but neither can I mobilise funds out of my salary for a lengthy stay in Cyprus, nor are there any foundations I can think of that will provide support.'

Martin smiled at Kamal and with excitement in his voice declared, 'No problem, I have a travel grant from the Royal Society which will cover all expenses. The only thing I cannot pay is your salary. I hope you will accept that?'

A week later, Martin and Kamal arrived at Nicosia Airport and after a lengthy taxi drive crossed the Kyrenia Mountains at the pass at St. Hilarion. The breath-taking views of Kyrenia below took both men by surprise. Soon they arrived at the Kyrenia castle and were welcomed by Mr Batzev, a young American, who was the archaeological leader of the expedition. The wine ship, dating somewhere BC, was still on the bottom of the Mediterranean, just off the harbour at 31 meters of depth.

18

Danielle waited for Alex outside the gate of the Akrotiri Airbase on the Akrotiri Peninsula just west of Limassol. He was expected to arrive on an air force prop passenger and cargo plane, the RAF Britannia but it was late. Delays on RAF passenger flight were common and Danielle had been warned. She settled down among the many spectators who watched the famous delta-wing Vulcan jet bombers flying roaring in and out of the airbase. At last, the Vulcan traffic ceased and a four-engine prop plane arrived. It had a characteristic nose making it easily recognisable.

It did not take long before an MP Land Rover arrived at the gate with Captain Alex William Sidney Smith. He wore civilian clothes but was given the full military honours by the MP officer and the guard at the gate. Before Alex passed the guard, he waved at Danielle. Outside the gate, Danielle offered Alex a full palm handshake which he accepted but he turned her hand and gave her a respectful but warm hand-kiss. Alex knew too well that women in France appreciate such a greeting. Danielle smiled and got behind the wheel of her jeep while Alex loaded his gear in the back. 'Big things, these Vulcan bombers are a bit scary,' Alex said. 'They may or may

110

not carry nuclear bombs.' Danielle released the handbrake and looked at Alex.

'Yes, it is, but it is nevertheless a spectacular sight.'

Alex appreciated the warm air coming through the open jeep as they drove towards Paphos. He could smell the sea to the left and the land to their right. Everywhere on the gentle slopes were vineyards and olive groves stretching for miles up towards the Troodos Mountains. He felt relaxed after bouncing in a prop plane along the military air-corridors of Europe. Danielle was concentrating on her driving and looked straight ahead. She could feel that Alex, once in a while, was looking at her, giving her a feeling she would like to avoid. She convinced herself that their relationship was professional, nothing else. Alex had difficulties looking ahead. After all Danielle was a beautiful woman and he accepted that he had missed her company. Alex tried to start a conversation. 'I am looking forward to meet the people from the Aphrodite Society of Cyprus; I wonder what kind of characters they are,' he said. 'Don't worry,' Danielle answered. 'I spoke to Lisa Lefkarides and I think she is quite a lady. You better watch out!' Alex laughed and smiled tensely.

They stopped at a roadside grocery shop. Alex bought two cans of cold soft drink while Danielle consulted her map. Back in the jeep they sipped their drinks. Danielle was still consulting her map. 'It's a bit tricky these roads. There are many small dirt roads and many without signs or names; I think we have to turn right after 4 miles.'

Alex kept an eye on the odometer and shouted, 'We are here!' But there was no road. Danielle kept on going and shortly after, a road appeared to the right with a sign saying "Villa Yanni".

'It's here,' Danielle said, took a sharp turn and sped up the hill. They drove for a couple of miles between the vineyards with their endless rows of grapes. Suddenly, a two-storey villa, surrounded by parapet walls appeared in front of them. There were olive trees and vines everywhere and up the columns supporting a sizeable upstairs veranda were Bougainvilleas in pink and dark red. On the wall were Passion vines and the smell of Jasmine filled the air. They drove through the gate. At the double door to the house, a beautiful woman was waiting. Her hair was black and she was less than 170 cm tall. She had dark eyes and was smiling. 'Eventually, we are going to meet,' she said and put her arms around Danielle before she had got out of the jeep. It was a mutual appreciation leaving Alex numb and silent. He walked the few steps around the jeep towards the door and Lisa shook his hand and said, 'Welcome, I have been looking forward to seeing both of you.'

Lisa guided Danielle and Alex into a spacious lounge with open French doors leading to a shaded veranda. At the doors, there was a breath-taking view of the coast and the sea, which made Danielle stop. She put both her hands to her mouth and exclaimed, '*C'est très spectaculaire*—what a beautiful view!' Lisa smiled and guided her guests to the left, where there was a spacious cane lounge arrangement. Lisa asked them to sit down and at the same time a well-built man with dark hair arrived in the doorway. 'Allow me to introduce my brother Avo.'

After a while, they all sat down and Lisa brought in watermelon and tall glasses with mixed fruit in sparkling water. Lisa sat down and said, 'Now we have to wait for Dewan; when he arrives, we will have lunch.' Within long a

112

limousine drove through the gate and honked the horn. 'Excuse me,' Lisa said and walked out. She came back with a tall sun-tainted gentleman in a dark striped suit. He had black hair with silver streaks. It was Dewan Affall, a UN diplomat.

When everybody was seated, there was a pause as if no one wanted to start the conversation. Then Danielle began, 'I have spent a couple of days at Aphrodite's bath. It was really fascinating. The flora there is exceptionally diverse. For a botanist, it's overwhelming. It was fascinating for the first time to see Serapias aphrodite, Aphrodite's orchid. I am looking forward to another visit; I am sure my report will impress conservationists.'

'Yes,' Dewan said, 'when everything is added up and brought together, we should have no problem getting all three sites within the fold of World Heritage Sites. They may exclude Aphrodite's birthplace because there is no archaeological evidence but I don't think it matters.'

Lisa turned to Alex. 'Alex, I believe that you have some questions for us?'

Alex placed his drink on the sofa table and said, 'I'm honoured to meet the leadership of the Aphrodite Society of Cyprus.'

Dewan broke in and quickly said, 'The three of us here represent the Society in Cyprus but there are two more—they are in Europe and will attend our annual festival which is soon due—sorry, I am interrupting you.'

'No worries,' Alex said and continued, 'I am searching for a large irregular pearl with a carved face of a man. The face was carved by the French sculptor Jean Baptiste Pigalle in the eighteenth century. The Society of the Priests of Saint-Sulpice commissioned Pigalle to use a giant clam shell, the largest species to make a holy water font in the Church of Saint-Sulpice in Paris. A lot of things happened in the troubled times leading up to the French Revolution.'

Alex paused and continued, 'The pearl was under the protection of Antoine de Phélippeaux, who fled to England, bringing it along with him. He joined my great-great-grandfather in the battle of Acre, where Napoleon was defeated. Unfortunately, Antoine de Phélippeaux died shortly after the battle and the pearl was brought to the Synagogue in Famagusta. My great-great-grandfather, Sir William Sidney Smith, then a Commodore in the British Navy and one of the famous undercover organisation leaders during the French Revolution, The Scarlet Pimpernel, was worried that the Ottoman Empire wanted the pearl because its original name was the Pearl of Allah. According to Sir William's correspondence, which is in the family library, he had asked the Aphrodite Society of Cyprus to seize the pearl at the Famagusta Synagogue and to bring the rabbi and his family to safety. The Society confirmed to him that the operation was carried out successfully. Sir William did not pursue the issue further because he believed that the problem was French. He was happy that the pearl was safe. Now, so many years later, things have changed. My government has had a request from the French requesting that the pearl be handed back. The problem is: Where is it?'

There was a pause. Then Dewan looked at Lisa, who nervously looked at her brother Avo. 'I suggest that you tell us what you know,' Dewan said, 'you are the specialist in history.' Lisa looked thoughtful and began, 'As I know it, the story is long and complicated. When Aphrodite's Temple in Paphos was destroyed by an earthquake in 350 AD, a lot of the records were lost. Of course,' Lisa said with a smile, 'your request, Alex, does not date that far back but there is a connection. Firstly, we do not know where the Pearl of Saint-Sulpice is but maybe there is a clue. Let me explain. It seems that the pearl and the clamshell were brought to old Suez by the Radhanites, a Jewish merchant clan trading in the Far East at the time of Marco Polo and thereafter. Somehow they obtained a large pearl which had a shape of a turbaned head of an older man. They tried to sell it in Muscat, modern day Oman, calling it the Pearl of Allah. They got into trouble and eventually sold it to the Venetians, who brought it to Venice. Then, Dodge Andrea Gritti gifted the pearl and the shell to King Francis I. So far so good. But there is another pearl.' Lisa paused for a while until Avo got brotherly impatient and said, 'Tell us, tell us.'

'Our Society dates back a long time. Homer mentions the sanctuary, the Temple of Aphrodite, in Hymn 5 to Aphrodite. At that time and long after, pearls were rare but not uncommon. The ancient Greeks saw pearls as something mysteriously divine representing female purity and beauty. In the ancient Greek text, pearls are called the Indian Stones of Love. When Alexander the Great crossed the Indus River, he was given an extraordinarily large pearl by a local tribe at Multan. They thought that the pearl would impede his thirst for conquest but to no avail. Before Alexander died in Babylon in 323 BC, he sent the pearl to Aphrodite's Sanctuary here in Cyprus as an offering to Aphrodite. The description of the pearl I have seen says that it is perfectly spherical, weighing 8 Mina's or about 7 pounds, measuring 8 Daktyloi, or a half foot; it will have to be an unusual pearl.'

Followed intensively by Arvo's eyes, Lisa took a sip of her drink and placed it back on the table. 'Now,' she said, 'after the time the Pearl of Saint-Sulpice was seized at the Synagogue, there are no records of the pearl's fate and that has caused some confusion. The sanctuary leadership believed that Alexander's pearl finally had arrived and treated it as an offering to Aphrodite. I believe it is the clue to its whereabouts.'

A lady appeared in the doorway and announced that lunch was served in the garden. They all got up and seated themselves around a large table shaded by the dense foliage of vine. The lady had set the table with delicious Greek meze plates, fresh bread and a few bottles of wine and water.

During the lunch it was easy for Danielle to have conversations with her host because her French upbringing had taught her that work is not to be discussed at meals. It is considered to be uncultivated behaviour. Alex was left with an impatient feeling he could not control. First of all, he wanted results and they were not forthcoming to his desire. The people he lunched with all knew that the British are inclined to force issues but Dewan Affall had no intention to dance to the English flute. After all, the actual ownership of the pearl was far from clear. He had already been informed that the Society of Priest of Saint-Sulpice in Baltimore was interested in the pearl because the ownership had officially been transferred to the Society in the US from the Society in Paris. They have documents to prove it. Dewan's interest was that of the Aphrodite Society of Cyprus and he was not going to hand it over that easily.

During the lunch, Alex asked Dewan whether he knew where the pearl was but he avoided to give an answer. Dewan felt that the question was rude and uncultivated. Dewan told him straight in his face but with the diplomatic finesse that a true Scarlet Pimpernel would never ask such a question. That comment made Alex silent and Danielle gave him a worried look. Dewan pulled a card out of his sleeve and said comfortingly to Alex, 'The only thing I can suggest is that you pray to Aphrodite like the Greek poet, Sappho, did many years ago in a plea to mend her broken heart.'

In a slow deep voice, he grabbed everybody's attention saying;

Immortal Aphrodite on your golden throne,
Daughter of Zeus, wile-weaver, I beg you,
Don't crush my spirit, queen,
With anguish and pain: but come here, if ever before,
Hearing my cries from far away,
You left your father's golden house
And came here with your chariot yoked,
And beautiful quick-winged birds led you over the dark Earth,
Fluttering their fast wings down from heaven through mid-air.

'It's a longer poem but she will come to you if you pray.' To laughter Dewan finished with a smile and drank a bit of his wine. Alex realised that he had a lot to learn if he socially needed to interact with well-educated people. He suddenly felt that his navy-time had changed him too much towards the military and that he had forgotten civilised manners. He decided to swallow his embarrassment, got up from his chair and said, 'I apologise and I have no excuse for my uncivilised behaviour. Allow me to complete the prayer, my prayer to Aphrodite.' Alex recited:

Soon they arrived, and you, blessed one,
With a smile on your immortal face,
Asked me what had happened now and
Why I had called you and
What I wanted more than anything to happen
In my crazy heart.

Alex looked up in the air and said, 'Here is Aphrodite's answer,'

Whom should I persuade now?
To love you? Who, oh Sappho, is doing you wrong?
For if she runs now, soon she'll follow,
And if she won't accept gifts, soon she'll give them,
And if she doesn't love now, soon she'll love you,
Even reluctantly.

Sappho continued and finished her prayer,

Come to me now too and free me from cruel
Cares and do what my heart longs to
See done and you yourself be my ally.

The room went silent. Smilingly, Dewan exclaimed, '*Touché*!' and laughter and applause broke out. They all laughed and smiled at Alex, who suddenly found himself a bit embarrassed until Lisa got up, raised her glass and said, 'You, gentlemen, obviously know your classics. I appreciate that. Let's bring a toast to Aphrodite and the excellent poet Sappho.'

After lunch, the company was again seated on the veranda. It was getting hot but a fan in the ceiling cooled the air together with a mild breeze that blew in from the sea. Soon, Greek coffee's kept the sleepy company awake.

Alex asked Lisa about the connection between Aphrodite and the Virgin Mary. She answered quickly, 'They are the same. The Virgin Mary is just an extension made up by the Christians. They took away her powers and made her humble but she is still Aphrodite. The early Christian Virgin Mary inherited from Aphrodite the functions of the queen of heaven, the Morning Star full of grace and the Lady of the Sea, the patrons of sailors. Even today, in many village churches on Cyprus, the Virgin Mary is being prayed to as Panagia Aphroditissa, the holiest Aphrodite.'

'I can see that,' Alex said, 'but how are pearls related to Panagia Aphroditissa?' Lisa looked at Alex, somewhat annoyed.

'Well, I have explained that. Firstly, a pearl symbolises purity and beauty. Homer, who is our earliest source, says that the reason for this is the Indian stone of love, a pearl, offspring itself of the waters akin to Aphrogeneia or akin to the Foamborn, which is an epithet for Aphrodite. Secondly, in Vedic texts from ancient India, pearls are born of the earth's waters and heaven's powers, fertilised by lightning flash. A pearl is considered to be a daughter of the moon. In Western cultures, the pearl has astrological associations with the planet Venus, the Morningstar. Like pearls, the goddess of love came from the sea. Due to their shape, pearls can have other associations. Some stories say white pearls are tears shed by the gods. One legend says the tears Eve cried when expelled from Eden turned to pearls. So, the relationships between Aphrodite and pearls are those of worship and admiration.'

Alex looked like a schoolboy who had been lectured but he just smiled and said, 'Yeah, yeah, I have got it now!'

Dewan and Avo laughed but they felt for Alex because they have also been the victims of Lisa's academic vexations.

Dewan looked at Alex and said, 'At the upcoming Aphrodite's festival, the Society's council will meet, as we do once every year, and discuss the issue with the Pearl of Saint-Sulpice. As the chair of the council, I will inform you about our decisions.'

19

After getting as much information as he could out of the Imam of the Abu Al-Abbas Al-Mursi Mosque in Alexandria, Charles travelled to Cairo and then to Al-Gurdaqa, where he intended to see Kamal Bashour. He felt that the Imam in Alexandria was not cooperative and thought the same about Kamal Bashour. Charles was angry and decided that he had been too soft. It was time to show people his iron fist. He had hired a car in Cairo and drove to Al-Gurdaqa rather than flying. It would give him a better chance of escape if he got into trouble. He was now carrying his 0.380 ACP Browning in a shoulder holster.

After carefully asking about the location of the fisheries laboratory, he found it 10 km north of the township. People did not know what he was looking for because they knew it as "The Museum".

The laboratory looked deserted. Outside the museum, garbage were spread all over the ground. The museum seemed to have few if any visitors and Charles disturbed two sleeping dogs who had feasted on discarded turtle carcasses. Goats ran freely and ate all sorts of paper they could find. There was no vegetation at all.

Charles spotted the building with the reception office. He walked straight in and frightened a young girl sitting in an office chair on the other side of a counter. She was dressed as a typical Egyptian woman in light colours with a hijab covering her hair. She rolled her office chair away from the counter. Charles asked sternly, 'Where is Dr Bashour?'

The young girl looked frightened and with some hesitation said, 'I don't know—he is not here!' Charles opened the counter and took a step towards the scared girl. She tried to get away but he grabbed her shoulder and squeezed it hard with his thump. She tried desperately to get out of his grip but in vain.

Charles asked again, 'Where is Dr Bashour?'

Tears were rolling down the girl's cheeks and she cried, 'You are hurting me, stop it!'

Charles continued, 'I ask you once more: Where is Dr Bashour?' He opened his jacket just enough so the girl could see his Browning.

The girl was shaking and said, 'I don't know. I think he went to Cyprus with an Englishman.'

Charles looked out of the window and saw a man in a grey tunic with a Kufi skull cap walking towards the office. He released his grip and pushed the door open straight into the approaching man who fell backwards. Charles walked fast to the road and sped off in his hired car. Rather than going back to Al-Gurdaqa, he continued north along the coastal road to Suez and drove fast, knowing that the Egyptian police could not catch him. In Suez, Charles bought fuel and proceeded to Cairo. In Cairo, he left the car at the hiring company. He had used false papers. The following day he was on an Egypt Air plane to Nicosia, Cyprus.

Charles found a small hotel in a side street to Metaxa Square. He laid on his bed until dusk, thinking about what would be his next move. He could hear the noisy traffic in the streets and the smell of burning charcoal reached his nostrils. He smoked a cigarette. When it became dark, he got up and walked out in the street. Neon lights were everywhere, advertising small bars and restaurants. He walked down Regina Street and looked at the lightly dressed girls in the doorways, offering him company if he would join them in the bar. *Whisky Girls,* he thought and walked on after giving them the glad eye. Further down the road, a couple of prostitutes tried to capture his attention but he was not interested. 'Maybe later,' he responded and walked on.

In another street leading from Metaxa Square, he found a bar. The name appealed to him. It was John Ogder's Bar. He walked in and realised that it was like a British pub, just what he wanted. He got himself a pint of beer and sat down at a small table along the wall. Carefully, he studied all the patrons who were a mix of military people and civil servants.

When the bartender brought him his second pint, Charles asked whether he had seen an Englishman in the company of an Egyptian. The bartender laughed and said, 'No, no. We do have a lot of Englishmen but no Egyptians.' He turned his back to Charles and disappeared behind the bar.

Over his beer, Charles read the latest edition of the English-language Cyprus Mail. There was an article about "The Kyrenia Wine Ship Excavation". He read the article with interest. He knew that Bashour left Marseilles for the Red Sea on-board Calypso to study archaeological sites. *Maybe this is where they are going, at least it's a chance,* he thought.

The following day, Charles was on his way to Kyrenia in a car he hired from a company opposite Ledra Palace, the most glamorous hotel in Nicosia. He had to pass the Green Line three times, slowly zigzagging between sandbag positions where UN soldiers with blue helmets separated Turkish and Greek Cypriot soldiers.

Charles enjoyed the drive up to the Kyrenia pass. He could see St Hilarion, the ruins of an old crusader castle. He didn't like all the coloured neon-illuminated white-painted concrete statues of the former Turkish president Kamal Ataturk, a common feature in the numerous Turkish military camps along the road. On the top of the pass, the blue Mediterranean opened up before him and below he could see the ancient Venetian port of Kyrenia. Charles felt a relief when he passed the Turkish checkpoint before entering the Greek Cypriot sector on the northern side of the Kyrenia Mountains.

A few streets up from the harbour he found a suitable hotel. After checking in, he walked down to the waterfront and found a restaurant on the western side, where he could observe the harbour entry next to the castle. It was afternoon, the time when holiday-makers flocked to the restaurants after a day on the beaches of the many small bays along the rocky coast. Charles ordered a Whisky-Sour and enjoyed the cool drink in the shade of a large parasol. He felt a sudden satisfaction when he observed a wooden motorboat covered with a canvas canopy. It carried six men in neoprene diving suits and among them were Junge and Bashour.

The following morning, Charles took the road east along the coast until he could see the site of the wine ship. It was easily recognisable about 1 km off-shore because a large barge carrying a white decompression chamber was anchored there. With his binoculars, he could see the name of the barge; it was Alasia. A dirt road led up among the olive groves to a small chapel. Here he could sit in the shade undisturbed watching what was going on at the wreck.

There were two teams of divers per day. Charles knew that the depth was a little more than 30 metres, which is the comfortable limit for divers using compressed air for breathing. By staying at that depth for more than 25 minutes, divers have to decompress on their way up to the surface. If they stayed longer, divers have to spend hours in the decompression chamber to get rid of the nitrogen in their blood. Charles had read on a poster outside the castle that the two diving teams at the Kyrenia wine ship spent more than one hour on the bottom. When the early dive team returned to the surface, they quickly dropped their tanks and, with a towel around their necks, were swiftly whisked into the decompression chamber. A tender locked the hatch and Charles could hear an air compressor start.

Meanwhile, the barge crew were operating a crane lifting a large tray from the bottom to the barge deck. Carefully, Charles observed the content of the tray. It seemed to be amphoras, some of them crushed. The crew on the barge packed the amphoras in crates and loaded everything in the wooden boat he had seen coming into the harbour the day before. The boat departed for the castle at the harbour entrance.

The boat came back with the second team of divers and among them were Bashour and Junge. He could even hear a loud American voice. After kitting up, the divers disappeared over the side of the barge, each with two large tanks of compressed air on their backs. Later, the first team came out of the decompression chamber. The motorboat transferred the first dive team to the castle.

Charles waited for the second dive team to surface. It took a while but they followed the same procedure and were quickly in the decompression chamber. He waited for the barge crew to use the crane but nothing happened. He noticed that a member of the barge crew communicated with someone in the decompression chamber through a porthole. Suddenly he turned around and made a circle with his right index finger. A crew operated the crane and slowly the wire and the tray was brought to the surface and lifted on-board. This time there was not much pottery. Charles could see what appeared to be two large mollusc shells somewhat encrusted and covered with grey mud. But there was more—a sizeable square-shaped item also covered with mud. One of the barge crew took a hose, started a pump and slowly washed the mud off. It did not come off without difficulty. The crew member tried to chisel it off using a hammer carefully but after some time he gave up and left it as it was. The collected items were packaged in wooden crates and shipped to the castle.

After watching the motorboat leaving with the crates, Charles got up and quickly walked to his car and drove to the castle. He wanted to be there before the last diving crew with Junge and Bashour returned. Visitors were allowed into the hall of the castle. He followed a guide showing his audience a large hall with crates of amphoras, planks of wood submerged in large tanks and lots of material on tables taken care of by several people. Charles saw the afternoon crates being loaded off the motorboat and brought into the hall. He was so interested in the incoming load that he didn't notice an elderly man standing among people a few feet away from him.

Much to Charles's disappointment, none of the archaeologists working on the excavated material took any interest in the recently arrived crates. They only worked on what was in front of them. A bell rang and the guide announced, 'The castle will be closed for visitors in five minutes. Please proceed to the exit.' With a deep breath of disappointment, Charles followed the crowd out of the castle, carefully looking for a way by which he might possibly re-enter on his own. He didn't notice that the elderly man had waited until all were out of the hall. The man crawled under a rope set up across a narrow staircase leading up in the tower and disappeared up the stairs.

At dusk, all the archaeologists, the last team of divers, including Bashour and Junge and Mr Batzev left the hall. Mr Batzev was the last one and turned the lights off. When everything was silent, the elderly man reappeared from the narrow staircase. It was Alex, a Scarlet Pimpernel in disguise. Methodically, he installed small cameras skilfully hidden from public view. The cameras had the same colour as the ancient limestone walls blending in among the stones and the grout. After having finished the job, he passed through the entrance leading out to the narrow dock. In the shadow of the wall, he was carefully watching a Greek-Cypriot soldier guarding an old submarine and two torpedo boats moored further out on the pier opposite. When the soldier turned around and slowly walked towards the sub at the end of the pier, a small black kayak came silently alongside. Alex slipped into the kayak and was quietly paddled away by a darkly clothed agent.

Later at night, Charles drove as close as he could to a small beach on the East side of the castle where the local country club had a swimming area. There was nobody there, and the restaurants in the harbour had all closed. He put on a black wet suit, mask and flippers and disappeared into the water. He swam along the castle dock. He had to be careful because of the Greek Cypriot soldiers guarding the navy vessels moored on the other side of the harbour entrance. There were two soldiers. One soldier was on duty and the other appeared to be his friend. They were sitting on the wall with their backs to the submarine and the castle, smoking cigarettes, looking over the sea.

Charles silently swam towards the excavation's moored motor vessel and dived under to reach the stern. He lifted himself into the boat with a push from his flippers. In the half-open cabin, Charles took off his mask and flippers. He watched the soldiers who were still smoking cigarettes. Charles slipped through the darkness to the door, leading into the corridor to the hall. He found the door locked. He pulled out a flat container from his pocket and took out a long slender tool. After a few minutes, he succeeded in releasing the latch and open the door. Inside, Charles started to search among the crates on the benches using a small waterproof torch. He found the one with the two mollusc shells. He thought they were too small to be the same type, as the one he had seen in the Church of Saint-Sulpice in Paris. He directed his attention to the square-shaped item, which was still in its crate covered by hard mud. With a small hammer left behind by the archaeologists, he tried to chip off the solid mud but it did not come off easily. He needed better tools and looked around after them. Then he heard somebody talking in the corridor leading out of the castle and the lights came on. Charles instantly ran towards the door to the castle dock but had too little time. He threw himself on the floor and crawled flat on his stomach, quickly hiding behind a stack of empty wooden crates piled up at the exit.

Three people had already entered the hall. They were Batzev, Junge and Bashour. They did not notice anything unusual but discussed with Batzev what the square-shaped item might be. After a close examination, Batzev said, 'It appears to be a vessel or jug made of black onyx but we have to wait until we have removed the mud. I will not do that tonight,' Batzev said and continued, 'If it is onyx, it might carry something valuable. Now, let us get some sleep; we have a long day ahead of us.' Batzev and his two companions disappeared out through the corridor, turning the lights off on their way out.

Charles got up and found the crate with the vessel or jug using his small torch. He thought about taking it away but it was heavy and there was no way he could carry it, let alone swim it to the beach. Finally, Charles realised the impossible of his situation and decided that he would wait until the archaeologists had opened the jug. He would check it out tomorrow night. Silently, Charles got back into the water and swam to the beach without being discovered by the soldier guarding the navy vessels.

When the castle exhibition opened for visitors, the elderly man was first. He skipped the tour and slipped into the hall where a couple of archaeologists were working. One of them worked on the square-shaped vessel, setting aside the pottery she had worked on the previous day. The elderly man asked the archaeologist whether he could take a couple of photos of the beautiful vessel. The archaeologist, a young female student, turned around to face the elderly man and said, 'I'm sorry but no. The item has not yet been released for exhibition.' The elderly man had a disappointed look on his face but asked again, 'Just one photo, please, it such a pretty vase.'

The archaeologist looked around to see whether anyone else was around. There were none, so she said, 'All right but be quick. I do not want to get into trouble.' The elderly man took a couple of photos, thanked the archaeologist many times and offered her a lolly. Alex walked along and the archaeologist turned her back to him to continue her work. Quickly he removed the hidden cameras. It was a relief for the archaeologist when the elderly man disappeared out in the corridor and left the castle.

After MI5 had informed Alex that Bashour and Junge had left Egypt for Cyprus, he posted several agents in Kyrenia. He and his agents stayed in a rented house a bit up the hill, overlooking the harbour and the castle. When Alex returned to the house, he removed his disguise as soon as he could. 'Bloody hot,' he said feeling sweat pearls running down his face and chest. After a refreshing shower, he closed the door to the bathroom and started to develop the film rolls from the hidden cameras. He looked through the black and white negatives before the film was dry and was excited by what he saw. As soon as the negatives were dry, he immediately processed the positives and hung them up to dry.

Alex looked at the photographs. He could not believe his eyes. First, a man in a dark wet suit appeared, immediately recognised as Charles. Alex studied the vessel or vase and thought it had to be something special. A photograph showed

Charles looking intensively at the vessel. He disappeared suddenly behind a pile of crates. Then the light came on and Batzev, Junge and Bashour appeared all studying the square vessel. Alex was thinking; he knew that the wine ship outside the harbour probably sank because of an attack. The archaeologists had found a spearhead embedded in one of the planks. The ship is dated to be from the 4th-century BC, the same time as Alexander the Great. *I will not be surprised if the vessel contains Alexander's pearl from India; it has the right size. I will inform Dewan,* he thought. Alex looked closer at the photograph he had taken earlier of the vessel and noticed that the lid was sealed by a copper ring carefully crafted to follow the neck and lid's curvature. There was an inscription. He studied the photograph with a magnifying glass and wrote the inscription *Αλέξανδρος.* 'I have to ask the Aphrodite people what that means,' he said to himself.

Alex made a phone call to London. He had to think forward and prepare and felt that it might be beneficial to have a fake pearl the size of the Alexander pearl available. He had to shout through a lousy connection, 'It has to weigh 7 pounds and be half-a-foot in diameter and I need it by tomorrow!' It was necessary to repeat the information several times.

Alex made a phone call to Villa Yanni and explained the situation to Avo, who was the only one there. With difficulty, Alex described the inscription to Avo, who had a hard time understanding Alex's description of the letters. When Avo realised that the letters might be the name Alexander, he got excited. 'The fake pearl will arrive in Akrotiri tomorrow afternoon,' Alex explained. 'We can only hope that nobody can assess the vessel.'

'Don't worry,' Avo said, 'let me take care of that.' Alex went below to his men, preparing them to guard the castle in secrecy.

20

The following day at lunchtime, Dewan arrived in Kyrenia accompanied by the Director of Antiquities. Dewan briefly met with Alex at the house while Batzev showed the Director around in the Kyrenia castle. Alex asked Dewan where Lisa and Avo were. Dewan gave a reluctant answer, 'They are busy planning the Festival.' It was partially true; in fact they were improving the security arrangement at Aphrodite's bath. Alex informed him about the progress of his plan, which Dewan previously had accepted. Dewan joined the Director in the Kyrenia Castle for a planned meeting with the leader of the wine ship excavation, Mauritz Batzev.

In Batzev's office above the castle's excavation hall, the Director went straight to the point. He congratulated Batzev for his successful excavation and recent find. He presented to him a document, signed by the minister, ordering the Director of Antiquities to confiscate a black onyx vessel found at the wreck on behalf of the Cyprus Government. It stipulated that the vessel was to remain in the castle until further notice, secured out of public view. The vessel was only allowed to be opened under the Director's supervision.

Batzev was furious but also surprised. He realised that he had been careless because the information had already travelled far. He had no choice. Batzev informed the Director that he had two guests, Professor M. Junge and Dr K. Bashour, who had discovered the vessel in the wreck, suggesting that they were entitled to know why. The Director rejected the request and said, 'I will report to my Government when we know the vessel's content. We will open it in privacy. You must not reveal anything to anyone about the conversation we have had. Now let's have lunch!' Two uniformed men from the Department of Antiquities removed the vessel from the excavation hall and brought it to Batzev's office and laboratory upstairs.

From the harbour waterfront, Charles had observed an official vehicle's arrival with four men, the Director of Antiquities, a well-dressed man and two uniformed guards. He saw them disappear into the castle. The two uniformed men revealed that it was people from the Department of Antiquities. It did not upset Charles because the department always kept strict control over excavations to avoid thefts and contract breaches. But their arrival indicated to Charles, what he already expected that they had found something valuable. An hour later, he observed three men who came out of the castle and walked to the café, called Costa's Café, on one of the bastions above the harbour. Charles left his seat in the waterfront restaurant and walked up the steep cobblestoned rampart to the bastion café, where he sat down a few tables from the three gentlemen from the castle. He wore dark sunglasses and had placed a camera and a small bag on his table, ensuring that a couple of colourful travel brochures were visible.

Charles was listening to the conversation. He realised that one of the gentlemen spoke in broad American. He guessed that he would be the wine ship's excavation leader. Based on their appearance he convinced himself that the two other gentlemen were Cypriots.

From the balcony of their rented house, with a pair of powerful binoculars, one of Alex's agents was watching the Kyrenia Castle and the harbour waterfront with all the café guests coming and going throughout the day. He saw the arrival of the official vehicle and the three men walking to Costa's café. Alex knew that the Director of the Department of Antiquities and Dewan would visit Batzev. The agent observed a man with dark sunglasses taking up a seat in the café, trying to look like a casual tourist. His light suit looked non-British and when he observed the man picking out a cigarette from a light-blue packet, he knew he must be French. The agent informed Alex of the person's presence at Costa's Café. Alex looked in the binoculars and confirmed that the man was French and that his name is Charles, a dangerous foreign agent. Alex immediately called Lisa and Avo at the house in Paphos but was told that they were not at home. Luckily enough, he soon got a call back from Lisa who had just arrived back from the Akamas. Alex informed Lisa about the situation and gave her the number to Costa's Café, asking her to warn Dewan. Alex and the agent watched Costa approaching the table with the three men. He disappeared with Dewan into the café. Soon after Dewan reappeared, joined the two men and sat down on his seat. Alex knew that now Dewan was informed.

In the afternoon, a white UN-marked helicopter landed on the helipad at the hospital east of town. Before long, the fake pearl was delivered to Alex in the rented house by a UN-uniformed MP-soldier on a white, light motorbike.

Two of Alex's agents had been watching Charles movements throughout the day. In the afternoon, he had left a waterfront restaurant and joined the queue to the afternoon opening of the castle. Charles was the first person in the line. The queue moved slowly through the ticketing box and into the castle courtyard. Among the other tourists, Charles passed through the doorway into the excavation hall. To his surprise, he found Bashour loading crates into the hall. Bashour immediately spotted Charles. Charles realised that he had been recognised and looked at Bashour with a stern face while pulling his jacket slightly to the side, enough to reveal a gun in a holster. Bashour grabbed an intercom phone on a table and dialled a single digit. 'It's Bashour. We have an unwanted person in the hall—please call the police.' Bashour's reaction took Charles by surprise. In a hurry, he turned around and left the excavation hall, pushing one of Alex's agents aside on his way out.

When Charles was outside the castle, he could hear police siren. As fast as he could walk, he passed the waterfront full of restaurant tables and chairs and ran up the cobblestoned rampart to the street above. Halfway up, he turned around and realised that two men were following him. Charles reached the top, turned right and ran as fast as he could. A door was open to an old warehouse. He walked in and closed the door behind him. A staircase led down below and Charles could smell that it was connected to a restaurant kitchen. All the restaurants at the waterfront were in buildings leaning up at steep rock wall, once carved out to form a semicircle characteristically for ancient Venetian ports. Charles walked down and apologised to the surprised kitchen staff. Out of the restaurant, he stayed away from the busy seating area and the open waterfront of parasols, tables and chairs, where waiters were busy servicing customers. He walked westwards up in the streets. He checked many times whether anybody followed him but could not see anyone. Back in his hotel, Charles packed his bag, paid his bill, loaded the bag into his hired car and drove out on the road to Nicosia. He did not pass the checkpoint but turned right to St Hilarion Castle. He found a place at the restaurant, so he had a full view of the road from Kyrenia to Nicosia winding up the hillside. He ordered a glass of red wine, lit a cigarette and waited.

The Department of Antiquities Director and Dewan were in Batzev's office when the intercom phone rang. Batzev listened in disbelief and said, 'I will call the police.' He hung up, grabbed another phone and dialled. When he got to the police station, he said, 'We have an unwanted person in the castle, please assist.' Batzev nodded a couple of times and hung up. He was not happy at all; he was furious. The last thing he wanted was to have foreign agents snooping around in his excavation paid by his Government. As soon as the problem with the vessel was over, he decided that he would immediately call his superior at the University of Texas, Institute of Maritime Archaeology.

On a table was the urn-like black square vessel now cleaned for mud. A copper ring sealed the lid to the vessel in a way the men found astonishing. How had the ancient Greeks made such a thing without making cracks or damaging the onyx? The copper ring was in one piece. 'It had to be moulded on the collar when the copper is very hot,' Batzev explained. There were no signs of soldering, and the ring was impressively smooth. The three men had an intense discussion about how they could open the vessel without breaking the copper ring. They quickly found the inscription *Ἀλέξανδρος,* which both the Director and Dewan recognised as "Alexander". But the cleaning process had revealed four inscriptions dividing the copper ring into four parts. It was *Παφία,* which the two men translated to "the Paphian", *Οὐρανία* "Heavenly" and *Ἀφροδίτη* which means "Aphrodite". They agreed that the three inscriptions were epithets for Aphrodite, indicating that the vessel was Alexander's offering to Aphrodite in Paphos. Eventually, the men discussed whether to open the vessel, but the Director was adamant; one way or another it had to be opened.

Batzev had a stereo-microscope set-up, so he could study the vessel under magnification. Throughout the discussions, he had remained silent because he thought that the Department of Antiquities' interference had taken that responsibility away from him. He was going to report the interference to the sponsoring committee, so it would not happen again; of this, he was sure. For now, he found that it was his responsibility to protect the vessel from any damage. Looking closely at the ring, he observed two small holes, concealed by the inscription *Ἀλέξανδρος.* First, he removed the mud which had filled the holes using a needle. With a fine painters brush, he cleaned the area using lemon juice. He washed off the lemon juice and had another look under the microscope. 'It seems there is a lock of some kind and I can see where the ring is joined,' Batzev declared in an excited voice, 'it's exceptional work, not easily recognised by the naked eye.' Dewan and the Director had a look.

'Allow me to suggest,' Dewan said, 'that if two needles are pushed simultaneously into the two holes, that may deactivate the lock.'

'We can try,' Batzev muttered in an unconvinced tone. He took two dissection needles and taped them together. With a fine calliper, he measured the distance between the two holes and bent the needles accordingly. Dewan and the Director looked on in silence when Batzev slowly inserted the needles into the two holes. Nothing happened. Dewan sighed and suggested, 'Try to push a bit harder.' Batzev glared at him and gave the needles a hard push. The joint opened a millimetre and with every push, it eventually came apart. Batzev carefully removed the ring, exposing where the lid joined the vessel.

Batzev largely ignored the two Cypriots when he carefully cleaned the locking mechanism. He was in no hurry. He studied the junction between the lid and the vessel and said, 'It is a hardened resin which holds the two surfaces together.' Without waiting for any opinion, he got up and disappeared up the staircase to the quarters above. After a while, he came back holding up a plastic container with dental floss. Batzev started to file away the resin, using dental floss. It was effective and he had no problem cleaning everything out. Oil was sipping out between the lid and the vessel but that did not bother Batzev. Patiently, he continued his work and with a brush sampled all the resin into a glass vial which he closed with a lid. Batzev looked at the two Cypriots with a wry smile when he attempted to remove the lid but it came off easily. He placed it in a pile of kitchen paper to absorb the oil and had a look. The vessel was filled with oil to the brim. He had a sniff and said, 'Olive oil.' He gauged the depth with a long, thin needle but a centimetre down there was metal. With a large pipette, he decanted the oil into a flask. Again with a wry smile, Batzev got up and with a pair of pliers grabbed something in the oil and lifted it up. It was a circular copper plate with a small handle. Four rods were connected to another copper plate and in between, a large perfectly spherical pearl was resting on a thick copper ring. They all looked in disbelief. It was easy for Batzev to lift the holding cage and take out the pearl. He dried the pearl with a soft cloth, folded the fabric around and placed it on the table. Batzev wiped his hands and said, 'Now it is up to you, gentlemen, to decide what to do. I think it is time for a coffee and later dinner.' Batzev locked the door to his office and the three gentlemen walked the short distance to Costa's Café on the bastion just outside the courtyard. The castle was now closed for visitors.

Lying down hiding on the castle bastion, Alex had watched with binoculars what had happened in Batzev's office. One of his men reported that Charles had left his accommodation and was now at the restaurant at St Hilarion, possibly waiting for someone. When Alex saw the three men leaving the office heading for Costa's Café, he quickly slipped down the stairs into the courtyard. A guard was doing irregular rounds, so he stayed in the shadow. Alex saw the guard on the northern wall, probably watching the harbour entrance where the navy vessels were, looking for another intruder who last time came this way. He quickly crossed the courtyard and entered the staircase leading up to the offices on the next floor. Batzev's office door lock was a simple one and it was easy for Alex to get it opened. He was now inside and locked the door behind him. He took the pearl from the soft rag and replaced it with the plastic one made in London. The original pearl was now safely in a bag attached to his belt. Alex was out of the door as quickly as he entered, locked it, and went down the courtyard stairs. The guard was still on the northern wall but had started to follow his route. Alex waited in the shadow until the guard had passed above before he ran up the stairs to the wall's western side hidden from the guard's view. He dropped a double rope down to his waiting agent and quickly descended. They rolled up the rope and drove to the house.

After having consulted with his minister, the Director, still in Costa's café, decided that the pearl should remain in the vessel. In his handwriting, he ordered, 'Refill the vessel with the lost oil, insert the lid, close and lock with the copper ring. Place the vessel in the office safe and have it regularly checked by the castle guard.' The Director would discuss the matter further with the minister and inform Batzev if there were any change in the directions. Dewan pointed out to the Director that his decision was not what he had hoped for and made sure that Batzev heard him. He would seek advice from the other guardians of the Aphrodite Society of Cyprus and with the Director's permission discuss the matter further when in Nicosia. Dewan pointed out that he believed the Society would insist on the vessel and the pearl to be a part of the Aphrodite Temple in Paphos when the restoration was completed. The Director shrugged off Dewan's concern.

When Mauritz Batzev returned to his office, he found Kamal Bashour working in the excavation hall below his office. Bashour had cleaned the two shells from the wreck and told Batzev that they were, without doubt, those of Tridacna maxima common in the Red Sea. 'It would have been a perfect offering for the Temple of Aphrodite in Paphos,' Bashour suggested and looked at Batzev.

'Could be, could be,' he answered.

Bashour continued, 'I am not a historian but it is tempting to suggest that the shells and the vessel we found were sent here when Ptolemy I was the pharaoh of Egypt. It matches the approximate age of the ship. I once read that there were a series of wars between Alexander's successors, where Cyprus came under Ptolemy's control. It would have been in his interest to consolidate his power here and nothing would be better than a generous offering to Aphrodite, the goddess of Love.'

Batzev nodded and said, 'Yes, but we can only guess. You better come up to my office; I will show you something.'

The two men went upstairs to Batzev's office where the vessel, the lid, the coppering and the pearl still were on a table as he had left them. 'The Director of Antiquities has just left and told me to put the pearl back and seal the lid to the vase. It will then be kept in our safe. I thought that you might want to have a look before I put the lot together.' Bashour was astonished to see the content of the vessel. The two men discussed the intricate locking mechanism of the copper ring. Bashour looked at the pearl and asked Batzev whether he could have a look at it under his dissecting microscope. He nodded, and Bashour sat down looking closely at the pearl through the microscope. He looked again and again. He was confident that there was something odd about the pearl. It was too perfect to be natural.

Bashour was thinking, pretending that he was still studying the pearl. He could not get himself to bring his assessment to Batzev, who had displayed a prodigious excitement when they discussed the find. He decided to keep his judgment for himself because he could not find any explanation of what he had seen. Bashour assisted Batzev in putting the pearl back in its holding cage, sliding it into the vessel, adding olive oil, and closing the lid. Batzev had a glass vial with fresh resin from an olive tree. He carefully smothered the lid's flange and pressed it into place, then mounted the copper ring and with the aid of Bashour's two fingers, managed to activate the lock. The two men carried the vessel into an adjacent room and placed it in a large, solid safe.

Charles waited at the restaurant at St Hilarion. He had dinner, but his expected guest had not yet appeared. A bit later, he could see a small car's headlights winding up the road to St Hilarion. The vehicle stopped at the parking lot and a man walked towards the restaurant. The man spotted Charles, now being the only guest. When the man approached the table, Charles leaned back with a smile and said, 'Professor Junge, I presume.'

Charles ordered a bottle of red wine and two glasses. 'I have some news for you,' Junge said. They opened the vessel this afternoon and the content was a perfectly spherical pearl, about 15 centimetres in diameter, submerged in oil. Junge took a sip of his wine, looked at Charles who was thinking, and continued, 'It is not the pearl you are looking for and I have no idea from which clam or oyster it came. I think it is better to leave it alone. There seems to be other interested parties in town but I have reason to believe that their interest has cooled. I think it will be more healthy for you to move on. I will suggest you look into the Aphrodite Society in Paphos.' Junge looked at Charles, who seemed to be speechless.

'Yes,' he eventually said. 'I think you are right. I can always return if needed.'

'Will I see you in Paphos?' Charles asked.

Junge nodded and said, 'I will be around.' After having finished the bottle, the two men departed.

A short time after, a rumour circulated in Kyrenia among the Turkish-Cypriots that the Pearl of Allah had been found and was now in the castle. It came to the Imam's ear and when he had one of his regular meetings with agents from the Directorate of Religious Affairs in Ankara, he reported his observations. The Imam explained that a guard at the castle had seen a black onyx vessel kept in a safe. The guard had heard that it contained a large pearl, similar in size as the missing Pearl of Allah.

21

Kamal Bashour sat at a table in a restaurant on the waterfront in Kyrenia Harbour. He enjoyed watching the life around him. He saw families with their young daughters and sons walking back and forth along the waterfront, enjoying a day out. They would not join the restaurant crowds but rather go home where the father would have a drink. In Cyprus, most young people do not drink in public, but going for a Saturday stroll is a family event.

Kamal planned to go back to Egypt and he and Junge had already finished their partnership. Junge had left Kyrenia two days ago. Now Bashour was troubled by his assessment of the pearl. *What if anyone had replaced the pearl?* he thought. It was not his problem. They had come to Kyrenia to look at the shells and finding the onyx vessel was just a little extra excitement. He was happy they had contributed to the excavation but the thought of the pearl would not leave him.

Bashour was sure that someone uninvited had been in the excavation hall during the evening and maybe during the night. But that was before the vessel had been opened and inspected. One evening, he had overheard the guard saying to someone that he had a feeling a person had entered the castle unauthorised, but he had no evidence. During darkness, it was not unusual that boys tried to climb the castle walls to jump into the water at the harbour entrance, a sort of manhood test. He was thinking about Charles. *He was certainly capable of such an action, but what about young Sidney Smith?* he thought. No, Bashour could not find a logical solution to the problem. He sipped on his lemon squash and looked across the harbour.

His eye caught a person that looked like the one he just had in his thoughts. He shook his head. *My brain is playing with me,* he thought and had another look. He saw the person walking on the cobblestone rampart leading up to the street above and out of the harbour. It took only a couple of seconds before he disappeared among other people but Bashour was sure that it was Sidney Smith. *He is here,* he thought, *it must be the Pearl of Allah he is after or the Pearl of Saint-Sulpice, as Charles had called it.* Bashour decided that he would go to Paphos and watch the Aphrodite Festival's processions, two weeks away. 'Surely, if someone is interested in a pearl, it must be the Aphrodite people.'

Ledra Palace is the most luxurious and glamorous hotel in Nicosia. Its restaurant is well-known for its culinary menu and famous kitchen chef. In 1963, a civil war broke out and Nicosia was divided into Greek and Turkish Cypriot quarters by the Green Line, named after the colour of the pen used by the United Nations officer to draw the line on a map of the city. The aggressive policies of the EOKA, a Greek Cypriot nationalist resistance movement, had failed. Their aim was Enosis, a union between Greece and Cyprus, ignoring the aspiration of the minority Turkish population. The final years of British rule had been a spectacular disaster, and many people on the island were happy to see them go. Now, the hotel was on the Green Line with soldiers behind sandbagged positions on both sides and UN soldiers in between. But the hotel prospered, providing accommodation to numerous UN diplomats and personnel. It was the site of many conferences and political meetings to solve the deadlock. So far, without any luck.

Alex's operation in Kyrenia had been successful and he and his agents had concentrated their efforts elsewhere. Ledra Palace's dining hall was impressive and there were many secluded places for people to have private conversations, a prerequisite for diplomacy and a meeting place for spies. British forces were a part of the UN peacekeeping efforts and Alex felt safe in Nicosia. Intelligence operations were mainly about the two opposing forces, the Greek Cypriots and the Turkish Cypriots. The only uncomfortable activity was that of Turkey, a Nato member. Most of the Turkish governments intelligence gathering activity was directed towards the British Sovereign Base Areas of Akrotiri and Dhekelia, seen as a threat to Turkish interest in Cyprus and the Middle East. Ankara did not see jet fighters, Vulcan bombers with their nuclear capability and British signal intelligence with friendly eyes. Turkey has not forgotten the Ottoman Empire's magnificence and has a nationalistic desire for its resurrection.

Dewan had invited Avo and Alex for dinner. They were seated in a quiet corner separated from other tables by a couple of portable room dividers and troughs with indoor plants. On a podium, a pianist was playing soft music on a Steinway piano. The three men enjoyed their meal. They had just finished the starter, a Lobster Thermidor and were waiting for a beef fillet steak. Avo and Alex did not know what kind of steak; Dewan had kept it a secret, a surprise. While waiting and drinking an excellent Cyprus red, Dewan directed the conversation towards the pearl Alex had taken from Batzev in the Kyrenia Castle and said, 'I will propose to you that until we have solved the mystery of the Pearl of Allah or the Pearl of Saint-Sulpice, the Alexander pearl should be kept in a bank vault under strict conditions. I have written a draft Memorandum of Understanding between the Aphrodite Society of Cyprus and The British Government. Both parties agree that Alexander's pearl should be housed in the Limassol vault in the Bank of Cyprus. Under no circumstances should the pearl be removed from the vault before a mutual solution is found and no third party should be involved. I believe that it is a fair agreement and I will encourage you to consider my proposal seriously.' Dewan handed Alex a heavy A4 envelope closed with a wax seal.

'That's fine with me,' Alex said. 'It's in line with our gentleman agreement. I will look through the document and get the High Commissioners signature.' Alex caught the attention of a waiter and soon a British UN officer appeared at the table. Alex handed him the sealed envelope. Avo looked impressed. He was not a military man but had been decorated for his leadership during the civil war. He was happy with his father's photographic business in Regina Street. His and Lisa's parents were Armenians who had fled from the murderous exploits of Kamal Ataturk in the aftermath of the First World War.

Villa Yanni was a haven for Lisa and Avo. When their father lived, the family spent time there during the hottest months enjoying the sea breezes on the vine-clad slopes of Mount Troodos. Lisa and Arvo worked in Nicosia and travelled to the villa for long weekends. Both were happy that their parents were safe there during the civil war. When their father died, their mother moved to London, giving Lisa incentive to spend more time at Villa Yanni because the villa and its vineyard were always in need of care. She hired local masons for maintenance and in the large vineyard there was no shortage of work.

Lisa enjoyed the company of Danielle. The report on Aphrodite's Temple Danielle developed was not complete without Lisa's knowledge. The Aphrodite Society of Cyprus had plans for a restoration of the temple to its former glory. The temple was destroyed by an earthquake in 350 AD. Lisa gave Danielle the Society's plans for a reconstruction which had been around for quite a while. Danielle was surprised to read that the architect drawings were already developed in 1824, 140 years ago. Lisa admitted that the plans were optimistic because obtaining funding had proven to be complicated. During the romantic period, in the first part of the nineteenth century, there was no shortage of ideas, only money. Lisa explained that the Danish-German architect, Gustav Frederich Hetsch was the only serious one. Hetsch had drawn up plans for reconstruction by using illustrations on coins and other archaeological material. He was a professor in architecture at the University of Copenhagen with substantial public building-portfolio in his name. 'Aphrodite's lure had a long reach,' Lisa said with a laugh.

Danielle's problem was to keep Lisa focused on the specific task to allow the three sites, Aphrodite's birthplace, the Temple of Aphrodite and Aphrodite's bath, to be UNESCO World Heritage sites. 'There are so many interesting things to look at, the Cult of Aphrodite is one but the Cult of Dionysus and of Aphrodite goes hand in hand; everybody likes a glass of Cyprus wine. Cyprus wine had been enjoyed for thousands of years,' Lisa ensured Danielle, as she showed her around an excavation close to the old Paphos harbour. 'A farmer ploughing the field here found a bit of mosaic and it turned out to be a splendid villa with gorgeous mosaic floors. There are several halls and rooms depicting legends and characters from Greek mythology but most impressively scenes of the cult of Dionysus. The archaeologists believe that it is from the Hellenistic period in the third century BC.' Lisa could not hide her enthusiasm and dragged Danielle across to have a close view of one of the most prominent motifs. 'Look at that, it is called The First Wine Drinkers,' Lisa said. Lisa again gave one of her many lectures on Greek mythology, 'The legendary Athenian King Ikarios, legend says, offered hospitality to Dionysus who in return taught him the secrets of cultivating vine and the making of wine. Ikarios produced the first vintage and was proud of his wine. On his way to town to give the first wine to his citizens, he met two shepherds and offered wine to them. They became drunk and thought that they were poisoned and so killed Ikarios, their king. Erigoni, the beloved daughter of Ikarios, sought her father everywhere and finally on finding his grave killed herself in grief.' Danielle looked at Lisa, acknowledging the interesting legend and said, 'It was not only the first wine but also the first casualty of excess drinking.' They both laughed.

From the balcony in Villa Yanni, Lisa showed Danielle their impressive vineyard while they enjoyed a glass of wine. 'From here, it's easy to imagine the sacred festival processions passing by with music, dance and song,' Lisa said and took out one of the many notebooks she had in a bookshelf. 'During works in the vineyard, we have found several interesting things which indicate that it may be the ancient vineyard linked to the En-Gedi described in the Solomon songs of songs,' Lisa explained. She opened her notebook and read, 'My beloved is onto me as a henna-flower in the vineyards of En-Gedi'. She looked at Danielle and said, 'According to Jewish history, the En-Gedi vineyard is believed to be in Jericho. The Hebrew texts mention that grapes from Cyprus were the most appreciated—I believe that these grapes came from here.' Lisa paused and looked at Danielle with a convincing smile. 'There is a link between the wine of Jesus in the Bible and the En-Gedi vineyard; the village here is called Engadi and I do not think it is a coincidence.' Lisa searched through her notebook, put her index finger at the desired page and said, 'I believe that our vineyard is the Templar's vineyard. It was here the Templars grew vines during and after the crusades. The Templars used prisoners of war as labours; they were Arabs and were called Saracen. We have found many small things such as belt buckles, pieces of metal ornaments and a few coins of Arabic origin.' Lisa opened the page where her index finger was and said, 'A 14-century traveller wrote: In the same province of Paphos is the vineyard of Engadi; it's like is nowhere found. It is situated on a very high mountain and measures two miles in length and breadth, girt on all sides with a lofty rock and wall, on one side it has a very narrow entrance and within it is quite level. In this vineyard grows vines and clusters of many different kinds, some of which produce grapes of the bigness of plums, others small grapes like peas, others again grapes without stones or grapes in shape like an acorn, all transparent and grapes and clusters of many other kinds are seen therein. It belonged to the templars and more than a hundred Saracen captives were daily therein whose only task was to clean and watch the vineyard and indeed I have heard from many of experience that God had made for the use of men no fairer or nobler ornament under the sun.'

'Don't you think this is interesting? Here, the Templars produced church wine which they considered the best.' Lisa cried out with excitement.

With an ironic tone in her voice, Danielle smiled and said, 'You have been to France, haven't you?'

22

Danielle had hired a business apartment in Paphos. The apartment was on the first floor and at the ground level were two large rooms where she could dry and press the plant material she had collected. There was also a tiny windowless room which she used as a darkroom to develop her photographs. She had an E6 colour processing unit to develop all the colour slide film she took right away. In a simple wooden press, she pressed and dried her plant specimens between sheets of blotting paper and mounted them on a thick A4 paper of a type commonly used for professional herbaria. She took close-up photographs of all the plants, dried, pressed or alive and mailed the prints to her supervisor at the Kew Botanical Garden in Britain.

She planned to travel to Nicosia and deposit the herbarium material at the Agricultural Research Institute but she allowed it to accumulate on shelves for now. She enjoyed Paphos and Lisa's company and was in no hurry to embark on a long drive to Nicosia.

There was another thing on her mind. It was that young navy captain called Alex Sidney Smith. It was difficult for her to get him out of her mind. Her work occupied her but as soon she had a break, he popped up as a joker out of a box. Danielle felt worse when visiting Villa Yanni because that was the place she saw him last. She thought about talking to Lisa about him. Lisa was older than herself and might have some helpful advice but she could not get herself to start the conversation. *It's childish,* Danielle thought. *Just get him out of your head.*

One afternoon she worked in the darkroom; there was a knock on the door. It took a while before she could leave the photographic material under development. The knocking got more intense. In a laboratory coat, she approached the door but stopped. The character of the knocking was annoying and did not appear friendly. Suddenly she got worried. She took a few steps back and shouted, 'Just a moment.' The knocking stopped. Danielle tiptoed to a window a bit away from the door and had a look at who was knocking. She felt uncomfortable and even afraid when she discovered that it was the same man who had shared her table in Roscoff. It was Charles. Alex had told her about him and had asked her to be cautious.

Danielle was not a woman without resources. Her father had prepared her well because when needed she would join the ranks of the Scarlet Pimpernel's, a family tradition. For her, it was an adventure but her father had not required her service except for intelligence gathering. In her lifetime, there had been no serious threat to the Royals of France. When Napoleon III was dethroned due to the Franco-Prussian War in 1870, her great-grandfather had accepted the various French Republics with resignation, satisfied with his grandfather's role in the crowning of Jean Bernadotte as the Swedish king, Karl XIV Johan, in 1818. Only occasionally, there was a need for the Scarlet Pimpernel's services and in modern time it was covertly requested by the French President or British Royals in cooperation with the British side. It was diplomatic missions by people well established, both in the private and public sector. Nobody would ever admit that they had met the Scarlet Pimpernel.

After the brief look through the window, she considered her option. The door was in heavy Greek style with two large iron bolts. She could ask Charles to leave. But she was interested to know what he was after. She decided to play a game and called out in a low voice, 'I am sorry but I am not presentable; what do you want?' Charles took a step back and looked at the door. He realised that any attempt to force the door open would be fruitless.

He answered, 'I just want to have a chat with you.'

Danielle asked, 'What about?'

'I have some information that you might be interested in,' Charles answered.

Danielle took a quick decision and loudly said, 'OK, twelve o'clock noon at the harbour restaurant tomorrow, the one with the Pelican.' Charles was not happy but he accepted that he had no choice. He thought about breaking in during the night, but Greek townhouses are like forts and there are dogs in the back yards. Everybody slept with windows open. *Such an attempt is likely to end in disaster,* he thought. He put on a French charm and answered fawningly, 'Miss Danielle, thank you so much. I will be looking forward to seeing you tomorrow.'

After having waited until Charles had walked away, Danielle quickly jumped up the stairs to her telephone. She called Lisa in Villa Yanni, got Alex's number and called. She got a military person, saying, 'Sidney Smith's office.'

After asking for Alex, the person abruptly answered, 'He is not available.' Danielle tried again but settled with the person's acceptance of delivering a message to Sidney Smith that she had called.

Frustrated, she sank into an armchair but no more than ten minutes later, the phone rang and a familiar voice said, 'Hello, sweetie, what are you up to?' Danielle explained her situation, avoiding appearing nervous but instead giving the impression that meeting Charles was a scoop. Having Alex ensnared like that was, of course, futile. He knew that she was anxious and dealing with Charles was not an easy task. *She needed back-up; why else would she call,* he thought. Alex was more than happy to provide it. 'Relax, sweetie, we are just around the corner and will be there on time. Ensure that windows and doors are properly closed if he should try to enter your house during the night. It's not to make you uncomfortable but it is a recourse to consider. I will dispatch one of my men at once. He will be watching your house until the morning.' There was a pause but Danielle did not respond; she thought about the complications.

She answered, 'When he comes, knock four times on the right side window and I will let him in.'

Alex smiled and said, 'He will.'

Alex briefed his men, jumped into a civilian car and sped off from the Akrotiri Airbase towards Paphos. He was smiling and thinking that Danielle, of course, knew that he would be that man. His men would arrive tomorrow, prepared.

Alex arrived after dusk and parked his car next to a vacant block full of discarded building materials. He immobilised the engine and set the alarm—just in case. He accessed his disguise gear in the car's booth and dressed up as an old,

156

Greek woman with a large, rough-looking nose and grey hair. He limped along to Danielle's house, making sure that there was no one around and knocked four times on the window. Alex heard steps down a staircase and felt that Danielle was checking on him from the side window. She released the two bolts, and he heard Danielle's voice from the other side, 'Have you had a sex change?'

'Only temporarily,' Alex answered. Danielle opened the door, pulled in a surprised Alex, closed the door and secured the two bolts.

Alex and one of his agents arrived in the harbour two hours before noon. He instructed a second agent to guard Danielle's house and follow her as she walked down to the harbour. It was measures taken to protect her from Charles. Alex was disguised as a Cypriot worker sitting in the shade, counting his worry beans. His agent was dressed in a Hawaii shirt with a camera, looking like a British tourist sitting in the café drinking coffee. Just before twelve, Alex, to his surprise, saw two men approaching the Pelican restaurant. It was Charles and Martin Junge.

Slowly, Danielle walked towards the harbour. She did not want to be on time as if she was eager to have the conversation with Charles. She had decided to make the meeting short because she needed to work. Danielle arrived at the Pelican some twenty minutes past twelve. She was surprised to see that the professor was there too. Junge got up and greeted her warmly, offering her a chair. Charles said with an irritated voice, 'I thought you said twelve o'clock.' Danielle ignored him, sat down, and placed her bag on the table.

A waiter served coffee's and Danielle asked, 'What's your business, gentlemen?'

Charles looked at Junge, nodded, and Junge began, 'I'm sure you remember the talks about giant clam pearls we had in Roscoff and I'm also sure that you heard about the Pearl of Allah alias the Pearl of Saint-Sulpice—we are looking for that pearl; we believe is stolen.' There was a short pause and Junge continued, 'Charles and I work for a US company called MESO with headquarters in Annapolis, Maryland, specialising in recovering lost or stolen antiquities.' Junge looked at Danielle as if he was expecting an answer or a revealing facial expression. Junge continued, 'Considering that you work for UNESCO, I trust that you will be interested or even committed to return stolen antiquities to their rightful owner?' Both Charles and Junge looked or stared at Danielle. Danielle stared back and saying nothing but it was obvious that the two men expected an answer.

'Gentlemen,' she said, 'I am sure that you have better things to do than to lecture me on my duties and responsibilities to UNESCO, have a good day.'

Danielle got up and grabbed her handbag, ready to leave. Junge jumped out of his seat, bowed towards Danielle, and quickly said, 'I'm terribly sorry if I offended you. It was certainly not my intention; please accept my apologies and please sit down.' Reluctantly, Danielle sat down, showing her dissatisfaction in her face and body language. Junge continued but this time with a slightly trembling voice, 'I have some information to offer if you, please, will assist us in this difficult task.' It was clear to Danielle that his servile approach was far from genuine. She asked, 'So, gentlemen, how can I be of any help?'

'You see,' Junge said, giving Charles a brief look, 'we have reason to believe that the pearl is here in Cyprus and that it most likely was stolen by a secret society of Aphrodite.' Junge looked once more at Charles, who had not changed his stern facial expression since Danielle sat down at their table. Junge continued, 'As I understand it, your work here is to prepare the necessary paperwork so UNESCO can reward the Cyprus sites of Aphrodite World Heritage status?' Junge looked at Danielle, expecting an answer.

She nodded and said, 'Yes, that is true.' Junge already knew her role in UNESCO, so Danielle found no reason to deny it. She guessed that he had got that information from her supervisor in Kew through the old boy's network.

There was a pause, and Danielle got impatient and quickly said, 'So what?' She could see that Junge got more and more nervous as the conversation progressed and wondered why. *I'm sure he is not telling the truth,* she thought. But Junge continued, 'We believe that the pearl must be hidden somewhere in Aphrodite's Temple and maybe at Aphrodite's bath. We will appreciate it if you inform us if you come across any information about its whereabouts. If the pearl is found, you will likely be the first one to know, don't you agree?'

Danielle looked surprised and said, 'I do not know from where you got that idea. I think you have too high thoughts about my role.'

Suddenly, Charles broke in, pushed his jacket aside, enough to show a bit of his shoulder holster and leaned forward saying, 'Miss, I don't play games, let me put it this way, if you do not cooperate, I will make sure your life will be miserable and maybe cease altogether—do you understand?' Charles nearly spitted in her face as he leaned forward.

Danielle got up, grabbed her bag and with a stern face said, 'You don't get anywhere with threats!' She walked away, but Charles got up in something that looked like rage and walked fast among the chairs and tables to catch her. He passed the agent in the Hawaii shirt with a camera, who stretched his leg out, making Charles fall forward and, with a crashing sound, toppled over among tables and chairs. He got up and grabbed the agent by his shirt, lifted him, and screamed into his face, 'You fucking idiot!' He raised his right fist, ready to punch his face, but halfway into the blow, his arm was grabbed by the Cypriot worker, who hard twisted it around. Charles fell-over face down onto the cobblestone pavement. Several waiters and a policeman, who happened to pass by on a small motorcycle, came running to aid but Charles got up and moved away, half running, passing Professor Junge sitting on his chair. Alex heard Junge say to Charles, 'You fool!'

Back in her apartment, Danielle had to sit down after having poured herself a glass of cool white wine from last night's bottle, which she had pulled out of the fridge. She had briefly seen the brawl in the café but swiftly moved ahead to get out of Charles reach. Danielle passed Alex's second agent, who moved out in the street to block Charles if he attempted to follow her. Now she heard somebody knocking on the door below.

The two agents and Alex and Danielle sat relaxed, each with a glass of wine. 'That man has quite a temper,' Alex said, 'we have to be careful; he is dangerous.' They all agreed and laughed about Charles' fall among tables and chairs. Alex praised the Hawaii shirt agent for his achievement and practical approach, rather than starting a fight with an unknown outcome.

'I have a feeling that Junge will approach you again, Danielle,' Alex said, 'because he did not tell you what information he has to offer. I think I know what it is but it will be good to get it confirmed. I think it's about Alexander's vessel, which he and Bashour found in the Kyrenia wine ship. He has seen the pearl.'

Alex took a deep sip of his wine and said, 'I also think you are in danger. Charles will go through with his threat to force information out of you. Staying here can be difficult. I wonder how he got your address, probably through Junge and then the Kew people—idiots!' Danielle did not say anything but sipped her wine.

After a pause, she said, 'I will rather not move somewhere else because I have to finish my work but maybe I can stay at Villa Yanni with Lisa for a while; there are people there all the time.'

23

After the incident in the Paphos Harbour, Martin Junge had had enough. It was clear to him that deeper involvement in Charles' enterprise would not produce any results. He had doubts that the Pearl of Saint-Sulpice, alias the Pearl of Allah, was stolen or whether the pearl in fact did exist. What really worried him was that every time they had made a move, Alex's MI5 people were there. Although he had seen a chance of earning money to supplement his meagre pension savings, Junge concluded that the best option for him was to go back to the drawing board to study the facts as a scientist, rather than to run around aimlessly like a headless chuck.

Junge met up with Charles in the café outside the small hotel in Paphos where he was lodging and told him his decision. Charles just shrugged his shoulders with indifference. Suddenly, it seems that he had changed his position. The Charles, Junge disliked, was suddenly back. Charles sat up in his chair moving his right hand across his chest and under his jacket, where Junge knew he carried a gun in a shoulder holster. 'You know,' Charles said, 'if I was you, I would be careful. You go home and study but under any circumstances I advise you to provide me with whatever you come up with, just in case.' Junge got up, preparing himself to leave and said, 'You haven't learned a thing—threats will not take you anywhere.'

Junge walked away with Charles, loudly saying, 'Just remember; I will come and see you.'

Charles decided to go to the local barber to have a haircut and his moustache stained black. He bought himself Cypriot clothes, similar to those he had seen the local workers wear. To the owner's surprise, Charles bought an old ute with a tray top full of buckets, shovels and an old concrete mixer. The owner didn't believe his luck as he saw his old ute rattling away while he was counting US dollars banknotes. For Charles, it was a perfect disguise presuming that nobody asked him questions in Greek. First, he checked Danielle's house but found it closed up with doors and shutters bolted from inside. Giving it some thoughts, he decided to wait somewhere along the road halfway between Limassol and Paphos. Charles knew that sooner or later, Alex would drive from Akrotiri to see his girlfriend and he would recognise any vehicle, even civilian ones if they were military. He found a good parking place overlooking the traffic coming towards Paphos. It was at the road leading to Petra tou Romiou or Aphrodite's birthplace, where waves break against steep cliffs and large rocks. One of Alex's agents reported that Martin Junge had packed up and left for Nicosia, presumable flying out and that Charles had changed his appearance, bought a workers ute and taken up a position at Aphrodite's birthplace.

In Villa Yanni, Danielle had many productive days. Lisa was delighted to see her and provided her with the working space needed in two rooms in an adjacent building, previously used for storage. During the evenings on the upstairs balcony, the two women enjoyed each other's company watching the setting sun over a glass of wine. Danielle casually brought up the subject of Alex, which bothered her. Carefully, Lisa listened while Danielle circled the issue without reaching the core of the matter. Suddenly, she changed the subject asking Lisa, 'Do you have a husband or a boyfriend?'

Lisa nodded and with a smile said, 'Yes, he is about to finish his officer commission in his homeland. I expect him to be down here shortly.' A rain of questions followed as if she saw Lisa's relationship as a life raft saving her from her problems. Lisa answered some but ignored others.

'Are you going to have any children,' Danielle asked intrusively.

At once, Danielle regretted her question when she saw the pain in Lisa's eyes. Lisa took a sip of her wine and folded her legs up on the sofa, looking comfortable.

She looked at Danielle and said, 'I can't have children. If I could, my parents were not likely to approve of my marriage with what they saw as an outsider. Cyprus is old-fashioned, particularly when it comes to women's freedom. I can't inherit any properties unless given to me. My brother will inherit everything, including me.' Danielle felt a deep sorrow and was about to cross the floor to give her a comforting hug.

Lisa quickly looked up with a smile and said, 'My father gave me the house in London where my mother now lives and also a good bank account. I also have a share of Avo's photo business. So I'm fine.' Danielle laughed with relief. 'Now what about you?' Lisa said, aiming to nail Danielle down on the question of Alex.

Now it was Danielle's turn to take her feet up on the couch, taking a sip of her wine. She felt the life raft drifting away and that she had got herself into a situation as if she was swimming in an endless ocean full of sharks. Eventually, Danielle came to some realisation and with her eyes looking on the floor said, 'I think I am in love with Alex but I do not know whether it is mutual.' To Danielle's embarrassment, Lisa laughed and laughed. She took a sip of her wine but got it into the wrong throat and had to cough in a napkin. When she recovered, she looked at Danielle and smilingly said, 'Don't you worry. I think young William Sydney Smith is hot as a hooting cuckoo. It would help if you remembered that he is British with a big B, not French. These Oxford boys do not show feelings before they are cornered but he certainly wants to impress you like a cock in a hen house.' Danielle did not know what to say. She was surprised by Lisa's straight answers. Danielle felt like a little girl lectured up by an older sister, and that Lisa measured her. The wine got to her head and she fell silent.

After a while, Lisa calmingly said, 'We—that is Dewan, Avo and I—have plans for both of you during the festivals. You will test Alex's intention. It's not that he necessary has any intention. He is confused but even more so than you are.'

Danielle again had to swallow Lisa's emotional superiority but hastily asked, 'Plans, what plans?'

Lisa moved her legs among the pillows to get more comfortable and said, 'You must promise me to keep what I tell you as a secret. We know you are both after the Pearl of Saint-Sulpice but it will come at a cost.'

Lisa paused and continued, 'Believe me, your love for one another will be tested but I am convinced you both will prevail but Dewan or Avo are unsure.' Again Lisa paused for a time, testing Danielle's patience.

Finally, she said, 'Both of you will have to retrieve the pearl yourself and replace it with the Pearl of Alexander. You can only do it through love and affection because you will enter the realm of Aphrodite guided by Dionysus. We have not made the final decisions but I believe it will go ahead.'

Lisa had to get up and get another bottle of wine. Danielle could not keep her tears back and went silent. Then she said, 'You must give some details.' In silence, Lisa poured them a glass of wine. It was Aphrodite's Claret.

Then she said, 'I can't give you any more details because I do not know what will happen but I can say that you both will voluntarily follow ancient trails joining the festival of Dionysus. It will eventually lead you to a sacred place where you may achieve your goals.' Danielle sighed and felt comfortably tired. Her eyelids were heavy, and she needed to lay down. With her head on a pillow, she instantly fell asleep.

Later, the phone rang and Danielle heard Lisa answer as though she was far away. It was a brief conversation. She heard Lisa saying, 'Yes, it's me, yes, Alex, yes, we will be ready.' Lisa hung up and within minutes she appeared in the doorway and said, 'It was Alex. He said that one of his agents is watching Charles, who spends his days waiting at Aphrodite's birthplace. He is poorly disguised as a Cypriot worker sitting in a ute with concreting gear in the back. If he leaves, the agent will follow him. Alex believes that he is waiting for him to lead him to the house.'

'I will go to bed,' Danielle said, 'I'm sorry that I fell asleep.'

Lisa looked at her with a sceptical smile and said, 'Don't worry, it's the wine. I knew that would happen. Sleep tight.'

Lisa left the veranda and Danielle went down to her rooms in the building across the yard.

Lisa was not up yet when Avo arrived. She got up to greet him, saying, 'What on earth? I did not expect you here before the evening.'

'I wanted to get out of Nicosia and could not sleep, so I decided to go. I left four in the morning—lovely sunrise.'

'Did you see anyone parked at Aphrodite's birthplace?' Lisa asked.

'Now that you mention it, there was an old tray top ute parked there. I thought it was odd.'

'Did he follow you?' Lisa asked.

'Why do you ask?' Avo said in an annoyed tone. He did not appreciate being questioned by his sister. Lisa explained about Alex's phone call and that a man called Charles may want to find Danielle and then she said;

'That's why she is here.'

'Oh, I see,' Avo uttered in a restrained voice.

'Maybe he did, I don't know.'

Charles sat in his ute smoking a cigarette. He was out of his favourite French brand, the Gauloises Caporal and had to do with the American Marlboro. It made him irritable. He had slept in the car on and off but there was not much traffic during the night. He was considering going back to his hotel to shower when he saw a van coming towards him with the rising sun behind. The sunlight prevented Charles to see what kind of van it was, but at the moment it passed, he saw the advertising on the side. It read: Regina Street Photo. Charles turned to see whether the van was heading for Paphos and to his surprise, it turned to the right and followed a dusty, dirty road up in the hills. 'I better check that. It's a bit unusual to see a Nicosia van that early.' He remembered the shop because he stopped there to look at the cameras.

He quickly started his ute and sped down the road to catch up with the van but he was too late. He drove up the hill with endless vineyards but no houses. After a while, he came to a side road with a sign, "Villa Yanni". Charles stopped, looked at the tracks in the dust and said to himself, *So, that's where he went.* He decided to drive further up to see whether he could get a view of the villa. He spotted the characteristically long slender cypresses and could see a small section of the villa but further up the road turned left. He decided to park his ute in a patch of low thorny macchia-vegetation and walk through to reach a rocky outcrop where he could see the villa. It was more difficult than he had anticipated. With his clothes torn in several places, he got to the rocks and sat down. With his binoculars, he looked over the roof of a separate low building; he could see the van in front of the main door. He heard the bells of a flock of goats driven up in the hills by a shepherd. Vineyards surrounded the villa but the area between the villa and the road was dense scrub. Charles decided to get a bit closer. He had to stand up to see the yard. To his delight, he spotted Danielle walking from the separated building to the main door. Charles knew he was in the right place.

It took time for Charles to work himself through the vegetation but he came down to the property at the back of the separate building. There were no low windows on the shaded site where he was but a couple of small ones high up. He stacked up a few rocks and was able to have a look inside. He could see a couple of long tables covered with plant presses, dried plants and paper. There was also some photographic equipment. He crawled down and explored the end wall of the

168

building. There was a low door, only four feet high and three feet wide. It was a classical pigsty door, allowing animals to pass between the stable and an outside yard. He got the blade of his knife between the door and the frame. By carefully moving the knife from side to side, he could open the door. On all four, he entered a dark room smelling of mould. Further in, he could see a door leading to the main room. When he was well inside, he heard someone enter the building. He looked through a crack in the door and saw Danielle approaching one of the tables and sat down on a chair.

Charles considered his options. He could barge in, taking Danielle by surprise or he could wait until she left, go in and hide, waiting for her to come back. Charles chose the last option and waited, sitting on the floor. It took time but Danielle got up and left for the villa. Charles stretched his stiff legs, opened the door and hid behind a curtain covering a doorway. He had his gun in his hand when Danielle returned. She sat down. Danielle sensed something move to her left and looked up. It was Charles with a gun pointing at her. She was shocked. '*Bonjour Mademoiselle*,' Charles said with a sleazy voice.

'We meet again.' Danielle froze in the chair. She was stunned but said, 'If you come any closer, I will scream!'

Charles smiled and said, 'Be my guest if you prefer to get a bullet through your skull!' 'Again,' Charles said, 'to continue our conversation at the harbour, I expect you to provide me with information about the Pearl of Allah as soon as it comes into your hand. If you refuse, I have no choice but to eliminate you from my investigation. Do you understand?' Danielle reluctantly nodded. She was busy thinking about how she could get out of this trap.

Avo enjoyed the large upstairs balcony view and walked between the pillars while Lisa was sitting on the sofa. He suddenly asked, 'Does Danielle have any visitors?'

'No,' Lisa answered.

'Well, she has now. I can see her talking to someone. The window is dirty but I am sure there is someone.'

Lisa got up, looked down and said, 'Oh, God, it's him.' She pulled Arvo back and out of sight. 'We have to do something.'

'Who is him?' Avo asked.

'You dickhead, I just told you. It's Charles, the guy who was waiting at Aphrodite's birthplace.'

Avo was cool as a cucumber, looked at Lisa and said, 'There is a pig-door at the end of the building. I used to play there as a child. That's probably the way he came in.'

Lisa quickly cut him off and said, 'I will call Alex.'

'No time for that,' Avo said in a calm voice. He knew that his sister was inclined to overreact.

'Calm down, let's think.'

'Keep watch,' Avo said, disappearing down the stairs and out through the veranda below.

In Danielle's studio, Charles was threatening her further. He was now standing in front of her, repeating his requests for information, but Danielle refused to answer. It was clear to her that he was getting more and more agitated. Danielle thought about what information she could give him. In a jerky reaction, Charles raised his hand and slapped Danielle hard. She nearly fell off the chair. She now got up and swiftly attacked Charles, swearing at him in French, while grabbing his wrist with the hand holding the gun. The counterattack surprised Charles, and even more so, when Danielle placed a right-hand blow straight in his face. He realised that he faced an opponent trained in personal combat. He grabbed her right hand with his free left, just to feel that she had her foot behind his ankle, and as she rapidly turned and pulled hard, Charles lost his balance and fell side-wards to the ground. He pointed his gun towards Danielle and shouted, 'Now this is enough—sit down.'

At that moment, Charles and Danielle heard a loud noise from the room at the end of the building. They heard someone encouraging animals to move. The door flew open and several goats looked in. More goats were pushing from the back and a flow of goats pushed quickly on, populating the entire floor space. Some even jumped up on the table, tasting some of Danielle's dried plants. Danielle forgot all about Charles and quickly removed the plants away from the hungry mob. Through the window, Charles saw a large male with a wooden club waiting at the door outside—it was Avo. His first intuition was to force himself at Danielle using her as a hostage but his experience told him that this might not be a good idea. He had no choice, looked sternly at Danielle and quickly said, 'Remember, I will be back!' Charles threw himself through the wall of goats, forcing his way through the door, pushing the shepherd aside and on all four crept through the pig door with goats jumping backwards in fear. His movements were a surprise, and Charles quickly disappeared up into the macchia-vegetation.

Danielle opened the door to the yard and pushed goats away, so she could get out, shouting, 'He got out through the pig door!'

Avo lowered his club, took a deep breath and said with no surprise in his voice, 'Good on him, that's where he belongs.'

Lisa came running across from the villa, shouting, 'Aren't you going after him?'

'No, what can I do with a man with a gun if I catch him?' Avo answered, providing calm to the calamity.

On the large upstairs veranda, Lisa had a look at Danielle's bruises. The one on her cheek was the worst one and Lisa gave her an ice bag to cool it down. The two women sat comfortably on the large sofa and Avo had made a large fruit platter and cool drinks to settle things down. He heard a vehicle in the driveway and got up. Down in the yard, Avo met a man who introduced himself as Alex's agent. He was apologetic and said sorry many times. 'It's my fault that he came here unopposed. I lost my concentration and suddenly he was gone. I'm so sorry.'

'That's all right,' Avo said, 'he is gone now. He disappeared up the hill towards the road. I think he has a ute up there.' Avo pointed. 'But he will be gone by now.'

'Thank you,' the agent answered and ran down the driveway to his vehicle.

24

It took a couple of days before Alex appeared at Villa Yanni. He was not in a good mood but apologised many times for his failings to protect the house. He looked exhausted, as if he hadn't slept for several days. Neither Danielle nor Lisa was warm in their reception of him but slightly cool. In their body language, they bluntly let Alex know and he could feel it. Avo had left the house and driven to Nicosia. They sat all three on the top veranda, watching the afternoon light and shifting clouds colouring the landscape with the many vineyards. They could hear the goats and their bells somewhere in the landscape. A cooling breeze gently moved the long curtains. Lisa got up and returned with a bottle of white wine in a wine cooler and a fresh fruit dish, dried figs and roasted almonds.

After they had sipped their wine for a while, Lisa broke the silence by asking, 'What happened to Charles?'

Alex mobilised his strength, got out of his languid position in the armchair, and took a fig. 'He disappeared,' he answered. Both women looked unsmilingly at him. Alex's eyes shifted nervously between the two women, realising that his explanation had left a lot to be desired. He grabbed another fig and washed it down with wine. 'He had left his hotel less than an hour after having escaped from here. We enquired the shopkeepers on the main road but first, when we came across the previous owner of Charles's old working pick-up, we made some progress. He told us that he had seen his ute heading up Palaikaridi Street towards Polis.' Alex crept back in his languid position while sipping his wine. He asked Lisa whether he was allowed another glass. Lisa smiled at his childish question and said, 'Please help yourself—there is more where it came from.' Slowly he leaned forward, took the bottle and filled his glass. 'Anyone else?' he asked. Danielle nodded and pushed her glass to the middle of the lounge table. Alex filled her glass.

Both women again looked unsmilingly at Alex, who continued, 'Unfortunately, he had a head start but we immediately drove towards Polis. We checked the tire tracks on the dirt road leading into Aphrodite's bath. He had been there all right but left again towards Polis. He did not drive to Polis but to the small fishing village, Lachi. We found his ute there, hidden in the bush, abandoned—it had a flat tire and no spare.'

Alex looked despaired and said, 'We made enquiries but nobody knew anything or were not willing to speak.' Alex paused and continued, 'He might be hiding in the bush but all his stuff was in the pick-up and crawling around in the Akamas is not for Sunday walkers. We could not find any tracks but only a few footprints, pointing towards Lachi.'

Alex continued with a voice of despair, 'While my two men were searching in Lachi, I drove to Polis to talk to the forestry people, telling them that an armed man might be hiding somewhere at Aphrodite's bath. I did not have that much information and the fact that he was armed was the only criminal offence.' Alex leaned back, feeling the effects of the wine and closed his eyes. Suddenly, he leaned forward as if he was afraid of falling asleep and said, 'The forestry people took notes and thanked me for the alert. I talked to the police too with the same result. They will let me know if anything pops up. After spending two days and nights on the edge of the plateau, watching people coming and going at the official visitor's site, we decided to call it off. One of my men was observing Lachi and, in particular, the coming and going of fishing boats. There was no sign of Charles.'

After a pause where Alex looked like he was thinking deeply, he said, 'Strangely, in Polis, outside the Forestry Offices, an old man who was sitting in the café across the square, approached me; he asked me whether I was looking for a man who had disappeared at Lachi.' He just said, 'The Harpies have taken him; it has happened before.'

After listening to what Alex had said, Lisa got up and went below to make a phone call. It was a lengthy conversation in Greek. Alex thought she spoke like in the navy—short commanding sentences. She came back up the staircase, sat down and said, 'Thanks for the information. I called Aphrodite's Guardians, who are currently training at the Stavros Forest Station in the Troodos Mountains to inform them about the development. They know the Troodos Mountain as their pocket; if he is hiding there, they will find him.'

'Aphrodite's Guardians?'

Alex asked. Lisa looked at him, shook her head and said, 'Who do you think picked up the pearl in Famagusta? I was an active Guardian for not that long time ago; now, I am one of their commanders.' Alex got himself up from his armchair and with a wry smile said, 'Cheers to that, you have my respect.' He raised his glass, stretched his arm towards Lisa and then Danielle, looking firmly at them and said, 'Ladies, you both have my respect. You do not need me; I know that you can take care of yourselves.'

Before Alex could put his lips to the glass, Danielle got up, jumped two steps forward to Alex and embraced him warmly, kissed him on his cheek and said, 'We appreciate what you have done, don't be such a fool.' Alex stood frozen in time and space, not knowing what to say or do. Lisa got her wine in the wrong throat.

A distant bell rang and Lisa said, 'Dinner is served at the veranda below,' saving Alex from further embarrassment. He nevertheless had a warm, comfortable feeling he did not fully comprehend.

When seated, they ate in silence. Still Alex did not know what had hit him. He was thinking about the fruitless search for Charles and felt he had failed. Lisa looked at him and Danielle from across the table and said, 'Remember, Dionysus' powers are manifold; he gave man the vine to cure their sorrows.' She stretched out and with a big smile filled Alex's and Danielle's glass. 'Now, listen,' Lisa said, 'we have to prepare for two festivals, the one before the other. The first will be the Festival of Dionysus and the next the Festival of Aphrodite. There will be many people for the latter but there will be far fewer for the former because this year, it is an arduous adventure in the Troodos Mountains, a trek that is not for the faint-hearted.'

Alex looked up from his meal and said, 'Do you expect us to participate in the Festival of Dionysus?'

Looking restrained, Lisa said, 'Not the lot but the trek in the Troodos, yes, I do, but it's the decision by the Guardians of Aphrodite. They have been in contact and they have made the decision.'

Lisa became more formal and stringently said, 'To enable an exchange of the two pearls, the Pearl of Saint-Sulpice and the Pearl of Alexander, you need to follow Dionysus. Otherwise, you cannot do it.' Both Danielle and Alex looked at Lisa, wondering what they had to face. Lisa looked worried too and between bites and frequent sips of wine, she said, 'Beware, you are going to enter ancient spiritual Cyprus in the mystical and ineffable Troodos Mountains. I advise you to stay strong and follow the flow. Do not depart from the company or go astray on your own.'

A car with headlights drove up the road and into the yard and parked outside Danielle's studio building. It was Dewan. He quickly ran upstairs and joined the after-dinner party of three. Lisa got up and gave him a kiss of welcome on his cheek. Dewan looked like he was in a hurry. 'Sorry,' he said, 'it has been a busy day and I just can stop.' Before sitting down, he looked at Alex and Danielle and said, 'I have two lots of paperwork you need to sign. The first is for Alex. It is a document that allows the Bank of Cyprus to release the Pearl of Alexander. The second is an indemnity and indelibly statement we all have to sign. The indemnity statement will free you and the Aphrodite Society from any liability if you lose the Pearl of Alexander. The indelible statement is a legal binding agreement between your government and the Aphrodite Society of Cyprus that the Pearl of Alexander will never be removed from its future resting place.'

Dewan placed the papers on a table, sat down on the sofa next to Lisa and said, 'Alex, you don't have to bother about the High Commissioner's signature—I have already got that.'

Lisa got up, fetched a wine glass, placed it in front of Dewan and poured him a glass of Aphrodite's Claret. 'Oh, thanks,' he said while looking up at Lisa, 'I need this.' He took a deep sip, and it was apparent that Dewan was stressed.

'Now, there is a catch. I have to ask you to sign the second set of documents before revealing where the actual resting place will be, simply because I do not know yet.'

Dewan looked even more stressed and in a serious voice declared, 'Lisa, Avo, I and the Aphrodite Society have put our fate in you. We trust and expect that you will carry out this mission, which of course, is also in your interest. As an offering, the Pearl of Alexander will change its name to the Pearl of Aphrodite when replaced with the Pearl of Saint-Sulpice. We do not know the exact location of the Pearl of Saint-Sulpice; only Aphrodite will tell you. That's why it has been safe for so many years. Sir William Sidney Smith knew this very well when he gave the Society the responsibility.' Dewan looked like a burden had been lifted from his shoulders.

Danielle did not know what to think and asked, 'Are you saying that you expect us to put our faith into spiritual powers?' Dewan looked like a worm on a hook and searched for Lisa's rescue.

'You may say so,' Lisa said, 'but it is not necessary the truth. Spirituality is a personal matter between the spirits and you and nobody else but you. I have advised both of you. When you have gained your own experiences, it will be much easier to discuss.'

Alex looked at Danielle with a smile and said in a calm voice, 'Well, sweetie, I think we are in for a real adventure.'

With a serious look, Danielle looked at Alex and said, 'The name is Danielle.' Lisa laughed while Dewan looked puzzled.

25

Chrysorroyiatissa is a Monastery dedicated to "Our Lady of the Golden Pomegranate", located high up in the Troodos Mountains northeast of Paphos. Since ancient times, Pomegranates have had a cultural-religious significance as a symbol of life, beauty and fertility. But they also symbolise power, blood and death. Pomegranates have always been the fruit of Aphrodite, appreciated as offerings by her followers for thousands of years. The Monastery was built on the ruins of a temple dedicated to Aphrodite and is now a place of worship of the Virgin Mary, Aphrodite's precursor in the Christian faith. The symbols of the Pomegranate is still an essential element in the monks' prayers.

Below the Monastery, there are several valleys and gullies. One of the valleys has a grove where the God, Dionysus, had been worshipped for thousands of years. It cannot easily be seen or recognised from the narrow road leading up to the Monastery. The valleys vegetation are dense with Cedars, Pomegranates, Myrtle, Cistus, Henna and old Oak trees. During spring, the valleys are ablaze with an abundance of Marigolds, Poppies, Mauve, Gladiolus, Blue Irises and in shorter periods, blooming orchids. In the valleys, the shy majestic Cyprus mouflon is grazing and above the rare

Eleanora's Falcon is flying, searching for prey. High above the lofty mountains, the mighty Griffon Vulture glides effortlessly with watchful eyes on animals and man. At night, the air is filled with a sweet floral scent and the nightingale's song.

Lisa dropped Danielle and Alex off at a small parking lot a short distance from the Monastery. Below high cliffs, a path with no signs leads towards the West, following the forested slope. Lisa kissed them both goodbye and wished them well. She quickly left.

Danielle and Alex could hear a bus labouring on the dusty winding road to the Monastery from the valley deep below. After a while, it turned into the small car park and stopped with squeaking breaks. About 25 people came off, most couples in their late twenties. They all had walking boots and a small day-rucksack on their backs. Their laughter was catching, indicating that spirits were high. The pilgrims were ready for a long hike. Most of them greeted Danielle and Alex, looking a little perplexed and asked how they had come up here. 'We got a lift,' Alex answered.

An attractive and graceful Cypriot woman got out of the bus and jumped up on a rock to look over the pilgrims. 'Please listen,' she loudly declared, 'I will guide you as far as the first grove, the one with the statue of Dionysus; this is the entrance to his realm. From there, you are on your own. Just follow the marked path further on. You are allowed to eat the ripe fruit you find on your way. Do not leave any garbage, please. After six hours walk, you will reach Paphos-Polis Road. A short distance north, you will find the entrance to Fontana Amorosa or Aphrodite's bath. There you will be met by a Forest Officer who will guide you to the bath. The return bus will wait for you there. You all have your maps; it should be easy. Come on, let's go.'

With the Cypriot lady in the front, Dionysus worshippers' procession walked two by two along the path following the slope of the hills. Soon the trail became narrow and they walked one by one, reducing the level of conversation. After an hours walk, a broad valley opened in front of them and the trail turned upwards, leading into a grove with overhanging vegetation leaving little light through. There was a limestone rock wall at the end of the groove and in front of it an old statue of a curly, naked man leaning lightly against a thick grapevine stock. The Cypriot lady cleaned green algae off the base, revealing the name Διόνυσος. Then, with a loud voice, she declared, 'This is the name Dionysus in Greek.' She took a grey stone bowl out of her bag and placed it in a hollow at the figure's feet. The worshippers had all gathered around the statue. She took a large handful of dry leaves from a paper bag and dropped them into the stone bowl. She sprinkled them with a brown powder. The guide looked at the crowd and with an intensified voice said, 'Please, bring out your bottle of wine and pour yourself a glass but do not drink.' There was a scrambling of glasses and bottles and a lot of giggling. The Cypriot lady again faced the crowd and held her index finger on her lips, indicating silence, which followed. She turned around and sprinkled a small handful of Pomegranate berries in the bowl. With a match, she lit a stick that started to glow, emitting an aromatic scent that spread out among the pilgrims. She placed the stick with the glowing end in the bowl, instantly creating a light, fragrant smoke rising from the bowl into the air and over the pilgrims. The Cypriot lady bowed and sank on her knees, raising her arms towards the statue and heaped lengthy praises in Greek while closing and opening her eyes. Suddenly, she got up and abruptly said, 'I will leave you now, enjoy,' and in a fast gait left the grove.

Danielle and Alex joined the worshippers in a toast to Dionysus and drank their wine. The smoke from the bowl made them dazed, giving them a sensation of cheerful lightness. They laughed, but Alex managed to grab Danielle's arm, and they moved away. Soon they had another glass of wine, sat down in the grass and watched many of the worshippers drifting into a mild trance in dance. Then, to everybody's surprise, a young girl gowned in light green silk, shrouded in an eerie veil of mist appeared at the statue and waving at them to follow her. She took the smoking bowl in her hands, held it high up and looked back to ensure the pilgrims followed. At first, nobody followed but then small groups did, leaving Danielle and Alex alone. Alex got up, took Danielle's hand and said, 'We better go along, remember Lisa's words.' They quickly caught up with the worshippers and joined in their happy trance and dance. They drank more wine, and the bluish smoke from the bowl reached their nostrils. It was unavoidable; it was as if the smoke crept along the ground, never raising.

Led by the young girl, the worshippers found themselves in another valley, more beautiful than the first. Flowers were everywhere with a deep scent permeating the air mixing with the bluish smoke from the bowl. The young girl led them uphill to a similar grove like the one before but without a statue. Instead, there was an old Oak with a trunk embraced by thick, creeping vines leading up to the crown. Similarly gowned in light green silk, young girls, wearing flower garlands, appeared smiling from the creeping vine branches.

They carried twig woven baskets, offering grapes and pomegranates, bringing along a strong scent of Myrtle. Then, out of the bluish smoke, which broke up their silhouettes, two strong hairy men came with long goat-like beards holding jugs and offering wine. The party settled in the grass, enjoying the wine, grapes and pomegranates to their heart's delight. In a trance, the pilgrims, Danielle and Alex, were spectators to a magical play, unable to resist the lure or decline the offers. But the allure gave them a feeling of immense happiness. Danielle and Alex felt a mysterious love and affection for one another. Alex attempted to steal a kiss from Danielle but she moved a little away, laughing with a luring smile. He laughed and moved along but kept a respectful distance, resisting moving too close. It was like a game.

Soon they heard a distant Pan-flute and listened. The crowd silenced as it came closer and suddenly a green-clad Pan appeared, easily recognised by his small size and pointed ears. On both sides of him were two beautiful young girls gowned in light silky green dresses, one of them playing the lyre and the other a flute. They danced and played among the worshippers who applauded and sent them air-kisses. Occasionally, a flash of sanity flew through Alex's head, wondering about the spectacle in front of him. He suddenly felt a deep desire to protect Danielle because she appeared to be happily unaware of the powerful allurement. She just gave him luring smiles and rewarded his kisses warmly. He thought it was a dream with no escape. The Satyr-looking males with their goat-like beards encouraged the worshippers to form a large circle, leaving ample open space where the young girls and the Pan played. Outside the circle, the Satyr's offered wine and grapes generously from what appeared to be an endless supply. The crowd was singing and chanting, following the music that grew louder and louder.

Suddenly, large birds appeared overhead. Alex thought they had a human head. He took Danielle's arm and pointed. Danielle nodded and said, 'Harpies.' It was the second time he heard this name and to his astonishment, a body came falling from above, landing in the middle of the circle with a hard thrum. In fright, Danielle turned towards Alex, holding on to his arm looking away. She whispered in his ear, 'It is Charles!'

Shrouded in a green mist, a muscular man walked into the ring, looking scornful at Charles, who appeared to lie lifeless. The man looked like the statue they had seen earlier. From the outer circle, the bluish smoke made it difficult to see clearly. The man looked at the worshippers and declared with authority, 'This man is Pentheus, king of Thebes. He has denied that my father is Zeus, denied me a place of honour and deity and declared a ban on my cult of worship throughout Thebes. My late mother, Semele, has been discredited and I have come down from the Mountain for vindication.' At that moment, Charles woke up, opening his eyes. With his face in mortal fear, he jumped up and, with all his force, climbed the vine higher and higher up in the Oak-tree to escape the man who had just spoken. The man's appearance changed and large horns grew out of his head. The inner ring of worshippers who could see the man clearly in the bluish mist fell forward with both hands on the ground louder and louder shouting, 'Dionysus, Dionysus, Dionysus.' Their excitement grew stronger and stronger as they watched Dionysus walking around in the circle with open arms. The crowd was going mad, screaming like wild animals ready to be sacrificed.

Desperate but encouraged, men climbed the oak using the vine as Charles had done. A mass of people was climbing higher and higher, surrounded by the bluish smoke, at last reaching the frightful Charles hanging on to the thinnest branches, kicking at anyone getting close. A man grabbed Charles's right kicking foot and another man his left. Aided by climbers below, the men pulled Charles out of his hold, and in the crowd's ecstasy, sent him scrambling down through the branches to the waiting Dionysus and his raging worshippers.

Danielle and Alex watched the spectacle from the outer circle, fearful of being drawn further towards the screaming crowd. The worshippers next to them screamed and tried to pull them forward to the crowd who, like predatory animals, threw themselves at Charles. Alex and Danielle looked on helplessly.

Two young greenish girls appeared each on both sides of Danielle lifting her. With their arms locked like in friendship, they guided her away from the circle and the frenzy. Alex got up and followed as fast as he could. With silky gowns fluttering around their bodies, the two greenish young girls guided Danielle forward along an open path as if they were flying. Alex ran and ran but as soon as he caught up, they ran further away. He felt the race went on forever and forever with no ending in sight. Alex became more and more tired, his vision blurred, his throat became dry. He felt overwhelming exhaustion. With his last strength, Alex reached Danielle and her two helpers. He reached out to touch her arm but one of the greenish young girls reached out towards him and pointed at him with her index finger. At that moment, just before his hand reached Danielle's arm, the greenish girl touched his finger. Everything turned dark and Alex fell and fell into infinity.

Slowly, Alex's mind woke up. He did not open his eyes of fear of what he might see. He heard splashing and flowing water, girls laughing and through his eyelids he saw flickering lights. He smelled Myrtle. He let his hand feel the ground but he could only felt soft leaves. He was on a bed of soft Myrtle leaves naked. He heard Danielle's familiar soft voice and laughter. Alex opened his eyes. He saw a cave ceiling with light reflected from water in a mesmerising kaleidoscope of colours. He lifted his head and saw a beautiful naked woman sitting on a rock in a pond generously supplied with water flowing down from the wall. She is playing with her hands in the water. A young girl is washing her hair.

Alex thought that this couldn't be real; it's surreal, it's surreal, he repeated for himself. The beautiful woman turned around looking at Alex. Instantly, he was stunned. It was Danielle, smiling at him.

In her lap was the Pearl of Alexander. She took the pearl with both hands and, with a leap, dived into the deep of the pond. Alex, subconsciously, jumped up and from a rock at the pond's edge, leapt into the bluish pond, following Danielle into the deep. He could see her deep down holding on to the pearl, using her legs for powerful swimming. Alex had to use both his arms and legs to force himself deeper because he had no additional weight to assist him. He felt the pressure in his lungs; he badly needed air. He saw Danielle on the bottom, resting on her knees. She was looking for him. Alex uses his last effort and reaches her. He grabbed hold of a rock and placed it on his legs to keep him down. He blows air out of his lungs and settles. He felt Danielle's naked body next to him. Alex tried to focus on Danielle's hands and Alexander's pearl. She holds it in one hand and starts to drift upwards. Alex holds her legs down. With her free hand, she reaches for an elliptic, unevenly shaped pearl resting on a pedestal. He realised that it was the Pearl of Saint-Sulpice; he saw the sculptured head. Danielle passed the Pearl of Saint-Sulpice to Alex. Softly, she placed the perfectly spherical Alexander's pearl on a pedestal.

Instantly, the pearl started to emit a strange lustre of white fluorescent glow. Danielle kissed Alexander on his mouth, blowing air in his lungs and with forceful strokes swam upwards. Alex followed. Weighted down by the pearl, he reached her. Danielle was struggling to get to the surface. Alex took the pearl in his left hand, grabbed her hand with his right and in sheer desperation forcing himself and Danielle to the surface. With his head under the surface, he pushed the pearl over the edge of the pond, allowing him to push Danielle up. He followed. Gasping for air, they both sit naked on the bottom of the low end of the pond in a warm embrace. Tears flowed down Danielle's and Alex's cheeks. They laughed and kissed them away. They got out of the pond and fell exhausted on the soft bed of Myrtle leaves.

After a short time, Danielle woke up. Alex said, 'We have to go; we have to go now before daylight.' She points at a small grape-collecting basket containing the Pearl of Saint-Sulpice. Alex grabbed the basket and pulled it up on his back while Danielle secured a support leather band around his forehead. Naked, they started to walk on the path leading away from the spring. They crossed the road and continued along the trail from which they had arrived. They walked for hours until numerous wounds and blisters prevented them from walking further. They rinsed their wounds in a small stream and tied thick leaves as shoes around their feet. They walked for further hours but had to stop to rest. Danielle wanted to carry the basket, but Alex refused. On the second day, they found the grove with the Dionysus statue. Exhausted, they lay down and instantly fell asleep.

26

Alex woke up lying in a bed covered by rough blankets. He felt Danielle next to him breathing softly. The bed was hard and uncomfortable. He turned over and woke up Danielle with a long soft kiss. She responded and opened her eyes. Light came in through a small window. There was only one door to the room, two small tabouret chairs and a small table. On the table was the Pearl of Saint-Sulpice.

'Do you know where we are?' Alex asked.

'I thought we were making love in Aphrodite's bath,' Danielle answered, 'but this is certainly not the place.' They laughed. Danielle looked around and said, 'We have no clothes, only these rough blankets.'

Alex covered his shoulders and sarcastically said, 'It is like the navy.'

Then there was a knocking on the door and a voice from outside asked, 'Can I come in?'

Alex looked at Danielle, who said, 'You are welcome.' The door opened slowly and a tray appeared. A monk carried it. A beautiful carved wooden box, a pot of tea, two large tomatoes and four pieces of bread were on the tray. The monk placed the tray on the floor, lifted up the box on the table, opened it, placed the Pearl of Saint-Sulpice inside and said,

'That fits nicely.' The monk placed the tray next to the bed and looked up saying, 'Breakfast is ready.' Both Danielle and Alex realised that it was Kamal Bashour.

They were stunned, unable to speak. Kamal went outside and came in with two bags saying, 'It's your clothes and two bags of toiletries. Lisa brought it here.' Kamal laughed and said, 'I guess you are both a bit confused. While you eat your breakfast, I will explain the situation if you will allow me to sit down.'

'You have been lost for four days. One of the elderly friars here found you when searching for truffles with his dog.' Kamal looked at Alex and Danielle, who wolfed down the bread and the tomatoes. 'You are in the Chrysorroyiatissa Monastery. In this room, Cleopatra lived her final years. It's the only structure that remains from the early temple of Aphrodite. It is believed that she was poisoned or had poisoned herself but that is not true. She wanted solitude after Mark Anthony's death and was weary of wars. One of her female servants took her place in sacrifice and she could incognito flee to Paphos, which she knew well.'

'What about you?' Danielle asked. 'I thought that you were a Muslim Egyptian?'

In a thoughtful voice, Kamal continued, 'As a boy, my parents wanted me to become a Coptic monk. I was enrolled in the Monastery in Alexandria at the age of six. The monks brought me up and during my youth I worked here in this Monastery. I met Lisa when we exchanged wine for blending. The Monastery always blended their wine with the wine from the Villa Yanni vineyard. Later on I studied biology in Alexandria. The monks wanted me to study the giant clams; I did not know why.' Kamal paused briefly and said, 'I think I should leave you to get dressed; we need to leave. The washing room is down the corridor.' He got up but in the doorway he turned around and said, 'We have had the police here searching in the forest down the slope. The dog of the elderly truffle-seeking friar who found you also found the remains of Charles. According to the police, he was attacked by a pack of wolves—we heard them all night.'

When the door closed, Alex snuggled up to Danielle and said, 'Why do we have to go? I could stay here for days.' She gave Alex a warm embrace and a deep kiss which lasted for a long time.

She tickled him until he said, 'Stop it, stop it.'

'No,' Danielle answered, 'we have to go, duty first, you know that. But thank you for four lovely, exciting days. I hope they will last longer.' Alex took his arms around Danielle, looked into her eyes, saying, 'Forever, seriously forever,' and gave her another deep kiss. Danielle smiled at Alex, got up and with a blanket around her grabbed a bag with toiletries and disappeared to the bathroom.

Dressed and showered, Danielle and Alex found their way out of the dormitory and waited outside in the shade of a large fig tree. Alex had his arm around Danielle. A dusty long black limousine came through the gate and stopped at the entrance. A uniformed driver got out and asked, 'Miss Danielle Laplace and Captain Alex Sidney Smith?' They both nodded. A voice came from the door behind, saying, 'Wait a bit, I am not ready yet.' The driver waved, went around to the back of the car, opened the booth and said to Danielle and Alex, 'Please give me your luggage.'

Alex looked at the driver and said, 'Sorry, but we have very little.' Danielle laughed. A few minutes later, Kamal came out, neatly dressed in a dark blue suit and placed a large travel bag in the booth.

The driver opened the back door and said, 'Please have a seat.' With the passengers comfortably seated, the driver took the black limousine down the dirt road from where he came.

Kamal said to the driver, 'Villa Yanni first, then Akrotiri.'

He looked at Danielle and Alex and said, 'Bishop's car, isn't it nice?' They all laughed.

When they drove through Villa Yanni's gate, they saw Lisa, Avo and Dewan waiting at the large wooden entrance door. Kamal looked at Danielle and Alex and loudly uttered, 'Uhhh, you are in for a warm welcome!' And so they were. Danielle and Alex could see that they were relieved and there were no shortages of hugs. Avo was over the moon and even Dewan, who usually kept his diplomatic distance, was nearly in tears, saying, 'I am so proud of you both. Thank you very much.'

Lisa gave Alex a generous hug and kisses on both cheeks and whispered in his ear, 'Thank you so much.' They all walked into the villa, Lisa and Danielle last. Lisa had her arm around her and said with a mischievously smile, 'Did you enjoy the adventure?' Danielle gave an initial little smile but she could not hold back her tears. Lisa had to take her aside and comfort her. 'Come on, dry your tears away. Everything went well; you were both marvellous.'

Danielle dried her tears away and said, 'I'm sorry, the whole thing has become too emotional. But how do you know?'

Lisa took a step back and said, 'Believe me, I know.'

At the ground floor veranda, a large traditional Cypriot lunch was awaiting them. It was difficult for Danielle and

Alex to hold back because they had not eaten a lot the previous four days. Over their black coffee's, Dewan got up and made a formal speech but this time far more private and emotional than usual. He ended his speech by saying to Danielle and Alex, 'I am glad you now have got to know Kamal. He has been a friend of the family here at Villa Yanni and, of course, myself for a long time. I'm sure you will agree with us that Cyprus is truly a mysterious island, Aphrodite's Island.'

Danielle could see that Kamal was looking nervously on his watch. Kamal got up and said, 'Ladies and Gentlemen, I think it is time to go.'

Danielle looked up and so did Alex and in a surprised voice he said, 'Where are we going?'

'Oh, you don't know,' Kamal answered. 'The Pope has sent his jet, a Learjet 60, to pick us up. We are going to Paris.'

Five hours later, Kamal, Lisa, Dewan, Danielle and Alex arrived at Paris Orly Airport. A black limousine picked them up and drove them to Hotel Ritz Paris. Five single rooms were pre-booked and paid for by the Society of the Priests of Saint-Sulpice. Alex looked somewhat perplexed but Kamal laughed at him and said, 'The Society always books single rooms.' He asked the Directeur de l'hôtel to change two rooms to one double room. With a smile, Kamal handed the key to Danielle and said, 'Courtesy of Aphrodite of Cyprus.'

For Danielle, the trip was a big surprise. Back in France, just like that. Then Hotel Ritz with everything paid. She was in a top mood, encouraged by Alex's attention and warm smiles. Of the five, Dewan and she were the only ones who spoke French fluently, followed by Alex, who could handle simple conversations. 'Maybe we can see your parents,' Alex suggested. Kamal looked nervously at his watch and said, 'There will be ample of time for you but for now, we have a schedule; we will officially return the pearl. The Society of the Priest of Saint-Sulpice expects us at the Church at ten sharp tomorrow morning. It is only a short walk across the Seine River.'

Dewan laughed, shook his head and said, 'Kamal, you are always nervous. It's first tomorrow.'

After a warm evening out in Paris at springtime and a long walk along the Seine, they found a small bistro, where they could enjoy dinner. Both Alex and Danielle were tired after days of mesmerising experiences, they did not fully understand. Lisa looked at the couple and with a smile said, 'Why don't you two go back to the hotel and enjoy a night in a comfortable bed?' To laughter, Danielle blushed and Alex looked school-boyishly shy. Grateful for the encouragement, they got up and thanked everybody. As they walked away, they could hear Lisa saying in a mischievously singing voice, 'Sleeeep tiiiight,' followed by more laughter.

At 10 am, they were all outside the Church of Saint-Sulpice. Kamal had a firm hold on the box containing the Pearl of Saint-Sulpice. In a low voice, Dewan said to Kamal, 'Lots of dark men with sunglasses.'

'Yes,' Kamal answered, 'the Church will not take any chances.' Danielle and Alex had shopped the day before to purchase clothes for the occasion because they had none. Danielle wore a beautiful dress suited for Paris in springtime, and Alex wore a dark, blue suit, his favourite colour. Lisa brushed with her hand Alex's jacket for imaginable dust and in the button-hole placed a red Pimpernel she had picked up from her bag. She then turned to Danielle and clipped in her hair a small rosette with a red Pimpernel in the centre, just above the left ear. Looking at the couple, it was evident for all that they were deeply in love.

The Bishop of Paris and several members of the Society of the Priests of Saint-Sulpice, gathered under the blue dome of the Lady Chapel, admiring the famous sculpture of the Virgin Mary with Child at the apse of the Chapel. A scaffold was erected to allow passage to the life-size sculpture. Except for them, there was nobody in the church and as they walked towards the Virgin Mary Chapel, they heard the large timber door being closed firmly behind them. The Bishop faced the company bowed his head and said a short prayer followed by an 'Amen' from the group. The box with the pearl was on a small table. The Bishop opened the box and called Danielle's name. Surprised and encouraged by Kamal, she walked over to the Bishop. He lifted out the pearl and passed it to her. With the Bishop first, then Danielle with the pearl, and a priest of Saint-Sulpice behind, they climbed the scaffold to access the area behind Virgin Mary's feet. A priest had opened Pigalle's pocket, and placed the lid pluck along the side. The Bishop looked at Danielle pointed at the pocket and said, '*Votre Plaisir.*'

Danielle placed the pearl in the pocket and stepped aside. The priest of Saint-Sulpice smothered marble paste on the sides of the lid pluck and pressed it firmly in place. With a soft cloth, he removed excess paste. He got up and with a smile said, 'When dry, it will be polished.' On their way back to hotel Ritz, they crossed the Seine at Île-de-France, where they found the old cemetery, Cimetiere Du Calvaire, and the sculptor Jean Baptiste Pigalle's grave. While the group was watching with their hands folded, Danielle placed flowers on the grave. A moment of silence followed.

27

Two years later a meeting was held at the Royal Society of London. The President of the Society was about to announce the winner of the £25,000 award for the "Pearl Biology of the Giant Clam, Tridacna gigas".

Spectators had filled the meeting room. On the first row to the left sat Dr Kamal Bashour nervously waiting. Next to him was Professor Martin Junge. Alex and Danielle sat further back. The President held a sealed envelope in his hand, seemingly enjoying the theatrical moment of the day. He was in no hurry. Eventually, he opened the envelope, folded out a piece of paper with a check fastened by a clip. The silence was deafening. The President looked out into the room and said, 'The winner is—,' a pause followed, 'Dr Kamal Bashour!' Applause broke out as Kamal walked up to the podium, where the President handed him a certificate and a check of £25,000. Everybody was standing up, applauding. Tears were running down Kamal's cheeks. The President gave him a tissue and pointed at the speaker's podium.

He had to go back to his seat to get his lecture notes but eventually faced the audience, saying, 'Thank you so much, I cannot believe this.' Kamal smiled and asked people to sit down. The room fell into silence.

Kamal began, 'I have examined three pearls believed to be pearls from Tridacna gigas. I X-rayed all three and determined their age using Carbon-14 isotopes. I applied gel electrophoresis technique to compare organic matter isolated from each pearl and living mantle tissue from giant clams. The three pearls are the Pearl of Allah, originally obtained by Mr Wilburn Dowell Cobb in Palawan, the Southern Philippines "The Sleeping Lion", once owned by Catherine the Great, obtained in southern China sometimes in the 1700s by Dutch. Finally, the Pearl of Saint-Sulpice presented to the French King, Francis I, in the early sixteenth century by the Dodge Andrea Gritti on behalf of the Venetian Republic.'

'Now, the results,' Kemal continued. 'The gel electrophoresis analysis showed that all loci investigated match those of modern-day Tridacna gigas. The probability that any of the three pearls do not stem from Tridacna gigas is well below 2%.' From the back, an assistant projected graphs and a table on a large screen. 'Furthermore,' Kamal continued, 'the X-ray analysis showed that all three pearls had developed nacre around a small jade nucleus at the shape of a miniature human head with a headdress.' Sighs of astonishment were heard from the audience when images of the X-rayed pearls were shown on the screen.

'About their age,' Kamal said, 'the oldest one is the Pearl of Saint-Sulpice dating 1470±72 years, the youngest one is the Pearl of Allah, dating 1870±72 years and finally the Sleeping Lion, dating 1630±72 years. These dates are the time when the animal applied the last layer of the nacre. I couldn't obtain permission to sample material from the nucleus in the centre of the pearls because of the pearl's value.'

'I have examined the shell which came with the Pearl of Saint-Sulpice.' The operator projected a close-up image of the shell on the screen.

Kamal used a light pointer and said, 'If you look closer, you can see a depression inside of the shell. I have placed the Pearl of Saint-Sulpice in that depression, turning it around for the best fit. Astonishingly, the pearl fitted into the depression with a tolerance of less than one millimetre.'

'Now,' Kamal said, 'I believe my results show that the legend of Lao Tzu is true. The legend is that sometime around 600 BC, Lao Tzu, the ancient Chinese philosopher and founder of Taoism, carved an amulet with three faces, Buddha, Confucius and himself, and inserted it into a clam allowing depositing of nacre to form around it. Lao Tzu transferred pearls to ever-larger clams as they developed, eventually reaching a size that only Tridacna gigas can hold. Since the nacre analysis is from the latest layer, I have not shown that smaller clams, possible other smaller species, have been used. Furthermore, the x-ray analysis showed that the nucleus is one head only and not three, as had been suggested, possible of Buddha.'

Kamal looked at the President of the Society, indicating that he had finished his lecture. The President got up and said, 'Are there any questions?' Lengthy discussion followed with an insatiable audience ending with prolonged applause.

Alex and Danielle had invited Kamal to dinner in their apartment close to Whitehall and the Admiralty. With two children jumping on Kamal's lap, Danielle asked him what he wanted to do with the money. After having organised the troops in his lab, he smilingly said, 'We do not pray to Mammon, Matthew 6: 24 and Luke 16: 9–13, you know. The money is for the poor and less fortunate; this is what we always have done.'

'By the way,' Kamal continued, 'the Society of the Priests of Saint-Sulpice in Baltimore has successfully challenged the presumed owners of the fake Pearl of Allah kept in a bank vault in Oregon. The court granted them ownership and the fake pearl is now kept in a glass safe at the Sulpician Seminary for everybody to see.'

Part 3
1974

28

A rainy afternoon on a spring day in April 1974, Alex returned home after a long day at work. He arrived at their house, not far from Whitehall. It was a typical London, white-rendered house with a low staircase leading up to the dark green main door with a polished brass door handle and letter slot. He could see his son's and daughter's faces piping through the white-painted window in expectation of his arrival. It was William, eight and Josephine, six years old. He opened the door and immediately they flew into his arms, his daughter shouting, 'Daddy, Daddy, can we play hide and seek?'

After a lot of cuddling and a swing around, Alex said, 'Can't you wait? I have to take off my coat and kiss your mother.' Danielle appeared in the doorway, greeting him with a big smile. Alex hugged her and gave her a kiss with his kid's still hanging on to his dark-blue navy coat. 'You go and hide,' Alex said, 'I will find you.' The two children ran up the stairs and disappeared into one of the bedrooms. Alex took off his coat, placed it on a coat hanger and hung it up to dry on a wall hook. Now he could turn his attention to Danielle and gave her a long kiss and hug before he slowly walked up the staircase. With one step at a time, he loudly said;

'They seek him here,
They seek him there,
They seek him everywhere.
Is he in heaven?
Is he in hell?
He is the elusive Scarlet Pimpernel.'

At that moment, he had reached the bed below which his two children were hiding. He threw himself on the floor head first towards the bed, stretched out his arms to grab them both. The kids were squealing with delight as he pulled them out while tickling them. 'Now,' Alex said, 'I hear your mum calling; we better come down.'

At the dinner table, Alex reported that he had got their airline tickets to Cyprus organised. 'We are flying British Airways to Nicosia, isn't that exciting?'

'Why are we going there?' Josephine asked.

'Have you already forgotten,' Alex said, 'it is going to be a big day. Your mother will present her work for UNESCO when the Aphrodite Temple and bath is declared a World Heritage Site.'

Danielle looked at her daughter and said, 'I have had a letter from Aunty Lisa and she is so looking forward to seeing you both; she can't wait.'

Alex smiled with a deep feeling of happiness and said, 'I have rented a house in Kyrenia. We can go there when the UNESCO celebrations are over.'

Later in the evening, when the two children were in bed upstairs, Alex said to Danielle, 'I think I might have to stay in Cyprus for a longer period than we have planned. There are troubles brewing. We have had information that the EOKA people are planning a coup d'état to remove President Makarios and appoint their own man. The Turks will never accept that and they are already planning an invasion. If we can, we will try to stop it but it won't be easy. I don't know what you think because we might be in the middle of it all and I am likely to spend a lot of time running around or in Akrotiri.'

Danielle looked at Alex and said, 'I am not worried. I have spoken to Lisa and she wants us to stay with her at Villa Yanni. It's not likely that much will happen in Paphos.'

Danielle went into thoughts for a while, then looked firmly at her husband and said, 'You know, I will rather be with you than sitting here in London worrying. If we are staying longer than planned, so be it.'

Alex smiled, put his arms around Danielle's shoulder and said, 'Still a Pimpernel, huh?'

29

Alex, Danielle, William and Josephine sat comfortably in a four-seat row. The parents had to organise time slots for each of their children to have the window seat. But after a couple of hours flying, William lost interest and allowed his sister to remain at the window.

Alex was reading an in-flight magazine. 'Did you know,' Alex said to Danielle, 'that you are not required to pay for your board and lodging when visiting Monasteries but you are expected to put an offering to the collection at the church. We did not pay anything; maybe we have to go back.'

'Oh,' Danielle said with a mischievous smile, 'you would like that?'

'Yes,' Alex answered, leaning his head affectionately against his wife's shoulder. 'I would like that.'

Danielle read Alex's magazine on the table and said, 'There is another good piece of advice; don't be surprised if an unknown person salutes you in the street. It is considered good manners if you return such a salute; remember that. Leave your stiff upper lip at home, darling.'

Alex lifted his head from Danielle's shoulder and said, 'Naturally, darling, of course, I will do as they say here: enjoy the hospitality of the Cypriot. Eat whatever he offers you, whether you enjoy it or not. If this is impossible, at least eat some to make him feel that you accept his hospitality. After eating that, I will go to bed.'

'No, you will not,' Danielle said with mild indignation, pushing him away from her shoulder.

The flight was not long and soon the excitement of arrival at Nicosia Airport started to build up. Danielle looked at her children and said, 'Our travel has not finished yet; a driver and a car is waiting for us. He will drive us to Akrotiri and from there, we will take another car. Your dad will drive us to Paphos. There, Aunty Lisa is waiting for us.'

In front of the airport, a limousine with a navy standard was waiting. The driver, a nervous young lieutenant in a navy uniform was standing at the driver's door. Alex and Danielle with their two kids in tow looked around. Alex spotted the limousine, pointed and said, 'I think it's that one.' He dropped their luggage and approached the Lieutenant, who was looking in another direction. Alex tapped him on his shoulder and said, 'Are you looking for me?'

The Lieutenant turned around and, with a loud voice, said, 'Commodore Sidney Smith, I am sorry, Sir. I did not see you.'

'That's all right. I will fetch my wife and kids. They are over there.' Alex pointed at Danielle, Josephine and William sitting on a couple of suitcases.

'Oh, sorry, Sir, I will get them at once.' The Lieutenant walked straight over, grabbed the bags and said, 'Madam, please follow me.' Within minutes, the whole procession was at the limousine, suitcases were in the trunk, and the family seated inside.

The limousine went straight through the gate at the Akrotiri Air Base. 'I think they are expecting us,' Alex said when they stopped outside the headquarters where a vice-admiral was waiting on the stairs. 'Hope you had a good flight, Alex,' he said and handed him a thick envelope. 'Please, install yourselves and come back as soon as you can; we have a lot to discuss.'

'Yes, Sir, I will. Thank you.' Alex went back to the limousine. The Lieutenant had already brought the family and their luggage over to a parked car. Danielle was on the back seat with Josephine asleep in her mother's arms.

It was dusk when Alex turned right and drove up the road to Villa Yanni. It was difficult for him to control his emotions when he saw the villa. When Danielle put her hand on his shoulder, he had trouble keeping his tears away. Alex could feel that Danielle, on the back seat with the sleeping Josephine, was overwhelmed too. It was nearly ten years ago that they were here last and he felt an unease. Two people were waiting at the door. It was Lisa and her husband, Erik. They smiled when they saw young William waving through the window.

After the emotional overflow of meeting each other once again had settled, they sat in the familiar sofas and armchairs on the upstairs veranda, feeling the light Mediterranean Sea breeze. 'I am sure you would like a glass of wine—am I right?' Lisa asked. Her question evoked relieving laughter. Soon a tray with sliced watermelon and drinks arrived and the kids settled down while they were munching away.

'Cheers,' Erik said, 'lovely to see you. I have heard so much about you both.' Lisa couldn't stop crying. Her husband had to comfort her.

'Sorry,' she said, 'it is just too much but it will disappear.' Danielle felt the same.

Early next morning, Alex prepared himself to leave for Akrotiri. He had a quick breakfast with Lisa and Erik. Danielle and the children were still asleep. Lisa looked straight at Alex and said, 'We didn't have time to talk last night; I have a favour to ask you. I need eight M16 assault rifles, four "Charlie G's recoilless rifles, 16 hand grenades and sufficient ammunition.' Alex nearly got his toast in the wrong throat and looked at Lisa. She quickly followed up, 'I need to arm the guardians. We only have four M1 surplus rifles, they are worn and it's hard to get the 0.30 ammunition. The situation has deteriorated after the military junta took over in Greece and the EOKA is getting noisy. We believe that there is a large risk for a Turkish invasion, most likely on the North coast.' Lisa paused but quickly continued. 'We have to be ready if an invasion force moves towards Troodos and Polis.'

'Do you know what these things cost?' Alex asked but he did not expect an answer and continued, 'Let me think. I may take it up today if the situation allows. In any case, I will probably be able to organise the weapons as a loan to the society, meaning that they have to be handed back if not required anymore.' Lisa and Erik nodded.

In Akrotiri, the intelligence officers met in the large meeting room. The Vice-Admiral provided a situation briefing, and it was grim. Essentially, the Americans would not allow the British to do anything because they were keen to please Ankara. The Turks were using the situation to their advantage. The Americans were not impressed but declared the Greeks themselves had made the situation intolerable, which was true.

Alex met with his commanding officer's office after the meeting had ended. 'Alex, I am happy you are here; you have many useful contacts. I know you are on leave but I need you; please, accept my apology,' the Vice-Admiral said while cleaning ashes out of his pipe.

He continued, 'Will you please gauge the situation and report back?' Alex nodded and thought for a while when the vice-admiral lit his pipe. 'I do need permission for an O45 requisition.'

The Vice-Admiral looked up, took his pipe out of his mouth and said, 'An O45?'

'Yes,' Alex answered, 'I need eight M16 assault rifles, four Charlie G's recoilless rifles, 16 hand grenades and sufficient ammunition.'

'Are you arming a new army?' the Vice-Admiral asked with a surprised voice.

'No,' Alex answered, 'this army has been around for a long time. It is very professional, entirely trained for covert operations and good at it. My great-great-grandfather used their services during the Napoleonic wars.' The Vice-Admiral nearly dropped his pipe and had to brush off sparks and ash from his uniform trousers.

'I certainly hope that they are not that old,' he said in a surprise reflection.

Alex laughed and said, 'I can guarantee you that—they are young and they are all women.' That information nearly made the Vice-Admiral drop his pipe once more.

He looked at Alex in disbelief and answered, 'You better give them some PP's as well; they are light.' The Vice-Admiral took a paper out of his right drawer and handed it over to Alex after he had signed it. Alex co-signed the document, handed the original back and folded the copy. He completed the O45 requisition and stabled it to the copy of the authorisation. After a warm hand-shake, Alex left the Vice-Admiral's office.

Alex drove out of Akrotiri Air Base following a light truck with a canvas-covered tray. A soldier was driving and there were two armed soldiers in the back. The two vehicles drove towards Paphos but they turned to the right going uphill towards the Troodos Mountains before the city. When they reached the Saddle of the Twelve Winds before Stavros Forest Station, four women in camouflage uniforms, armed with light rifles, were waiting. They welcomed Alex and the soldiers. The three soldiers and three armed women were left at Alex's car. The commanding officer instructed Alex to drive the truck and she jumped onto the passenger seat. She guided Alex further along the road until they reached the foot of Tripylos, from where they could see far over the Morphou Plain to the Kyrenia Mountains. Alex, driving the truck, was directed through a narrow road that zigzagged through the forest, along steep mountain slopes, before reaching an end. The road forward was blocked by large boulders. There, Lisa was waiting dressed in uniform. Several uniformed women came out and began to carry boxes from the back of the truck to four waiting donkeys. Lisa kissed Alex on the cheek and said, 'I cannot thank you enough for this; we are so grateful. You better drive back to the waiting soldiers. Allow them to leave in the truck. Wait there and I will pick you up and show you around.'

After the soldiers have left, the three guardians followed their progress down the road until they reached the main road. One of the guardians stayed behind with Alex's car while the remaining two brought out three donkeys from the forest. Riding on donkeys, the party travelled back to the place where Alex had left Lisa.

Lisa again met Alex and said, 'We have decided to show you the facilities to convince you of our capability. We want to reciprocate the trust you have given us.' Lisa guided Alex through a network of tunnels opening up on a mountainside, providing a spectacular view of the Kyrenia Mountain Range and Nicosia. There were many optical instruments, including large night binoculars. There were numerous hidden sniper posts. Lisa showed him their quarters with carved walls showing goddesses, Dryads, three nymphs, Satyrs and flying Harpies. Lisa could not tell him how old they were. Alex was impressed with the discipline, agility and fitness of the Guardians. Lisa explained that the site was only one of many throughout the Troodos Mountain Range. Their weapon depot was impressive but ancient. Lisa showed him weapons from Alexander the Great's time, maintained in a quality he had never seen before. Alex thought about the four nights he had spent with Danielle in the forest and the Akamas, wondering whether he would ever be able to explain the experience. Lisa read his thoughts and said, 'Cyprus is a magical place, don't try to rationalise—you will lose yourself.'

'Come this way, the girls are ready,' Lisa said and guided Alex into a classroom. Several camouflage-uniformed Guardians were standing in attention, and on a table was an M16 automatic assault rifle, one Charlie G's recoilless rifle and a Walter PP handgun. Alex asked Lisa where the black tube was. 'Oh, sorry, I will get it.' Alex asked the class to sit down. He realised that the women were of many different nationalities, most of the Middle-Eastern appearance but they all spoke fluently English. Alex explained the Walter PP pistol and the M16 assault rifle function but quickly learned that the class had experience way beyond his expectation. They were only interested in Charlie G. He changed his approach and asked them to circle the table. He lifted the tube-like weapon and explained, 'This is a well-tested Swedish made weapon. The Swedes call it Carl Gustaf because of the name of the original manufacturer. In Britain, we call it Charlie G. It can use various ammunition from anti-tank to personnel grenades. We have provided you with several types, enough to stop an armoured infantry unit in its track.'

'Then there is this one,' Alex said and took the black tube, opened in one end and pulled out a long slim tube with optics in one end and closed in the other. It had a rifle scope on top, a handgrip and a carrying strap. 'This is a powerful laser gun. It is an experimental version, which I found in our depot. It was to be destroyed, so I got it. I believe it will be handy.'

'Let me explain,' Alex said while taking it on his shoulder. 'I am not going to activate it here but later at the rifle range. At an aircraft attack,' Alex continued, 'You point the laser towards an incoming plane and fire a couple of times. It will be electronically registered on the aircraft as if a laser-guided missile had been fired and the pilot will most likely abort the attack. There are no aircraft of importance under control of the Cypriot government and a likely attack will be Turkish.'

Alex moved to practise aiming and loading, explaining all the security requirements. Later he used a couple of hours with the women on a small shooting range hidden between rock formations. Lisa observed the women's progress with satisfaction. Alex turned to Lisa and said, 'No more live practise with the Charlie-G; each round costs at least $500!'

30

Danielle, Alex, Josephine and William spent two weeks in Villa Janni with Lisa and Erik before driving to Kyrenia to occupy the house waiting for them. The situation in Cyprus appeared calm, allowing Alex to assume his intended vacation. In Kyrenia, they spent time on Six-mile Beach, enjoying the sun and water. During the weekend, Lisa, Avo and Erik came to Kyrenia and stayed with them. They rented a motorboat, dived and snorkelled leisurely around Snake Island. When they left the harbour, Alex noted that the ageing, small submarine had disappeared, but the two torpedo-boats were still there. He recognised them as American WWII surplus, and they looked like being in order. Two armed Cypriot soldiers guarded them.

In the evening, they had dinner at Costa's restaurant on the castle bastion. There they again met Mauritz Batzev and his wife having dinner. Batzev seemed happy with the Kyrenia wine ship excavation progress and there was no mention of Alexander's vessel. 'The entire wreck is now in the castle submerged in large tanks,' Batzev explained, 'and later on, the timber will be treated with polyethylene glycol or PEG, which penetrates the wood, eventually turning into wax-like substance. It is a long process but we will get there. In the end, the wreck will be assembled and put on display in the castle.' They all congratulated Batzev and his wife on their success.

On the 15 of July, Danielle walked to the baker in the street where their rented house was and saw a crowd gathered in a small café reaching out in the street. As usual, the television was on but the volume was much higher than it used to be. She stopped and watched. A news-reader was on the screen speaking in Greek. Danielle asked a man what the fuss was all about. Still, with his eyes fixed on the screen, he said, 'The Cypriot National Guard and the EOKA, led by the Greek Junta, have launched a coup. They have overthrown our President, Archbishop Makarios. Now they are rambling about Enosis.' He looked at Danielle and she could see there were tears in his eyes but in the café, people were celebrating.

He turned towards the celebrating crowd and said, 'They are fools; now we are doomed.'

With two loaves of bread under her arm, Danielle ran as fast as she could back to the house, barged through the door shouting, 'Alex, the Junta has done it!' Alex immediately ran for the post office to call the Vice-Admiral in Akrotiri. 'Stay put and wait,' was his order. He called Lisa and Erik but got only Erik on the phone. 'She left early this morning. We are aware of the situation, and we can only hope for the best. President Makarios will address the UN-security Council on the 19th and until then, it is not likely anything will happen.'

'That's only three days away,' Alex said.

'Alex, calm down; this is Cyprus. Prepare yourself like everybody else is doing.'

Throughout the night, every inhabitant of Kyrenia was watching television to hear President Makarios's speech in the UN-security council. Danielle and Alex did not sleep much because of the loud TV volume from the café. There was an eerie silence among the spectators. Early morning, the television news repeated Markarios' speech over and over again. Alex heard him saying forcefully, 'The coup of the Greek junta is an invasion and from its consequences the whole people of Cyprus suffers both Greeks and Turks.'

In the late afternoon, the owner of the café, two blocks down, knocked on their door. He carried a tray with two short blacks, two glasses of lemonade and a plate with four syrup-pickled green walnuts. Danielle opened the door and the café owner said, 'Your husband must call Akrotiri at once—they told me so on the phone.' Alex rushed to the post office because there he could talk in an insulated phone boot. He got the Vice-Admiral on the line. It was a brief conversation, 'Alex,' he said, 'an invasion force has left the South Coast of Turkey, heading towards Cyprus. We believe their target is Kyrenia—be ready to evacuate.'

Alex rushed back to the house to Danielle and said, 'We better pack the car; the Turks will be here tomorrow.'

'Do you want to leave now?' Danielle asked.

'No,' Alex answered, 'but let us be prepared.'

Early in the morning, Alex drove up to Bellapais, where he could get a clear view over the sea. He scanned the horizon and towards the Turkish coastline with his binoculars, which could be seen in the distance. There was nothing to see, so he searched towards the East. Suddenly, Alex saw something and reflexively stood up and sure enough, black dots of numerous vessels appeared in his view. On his way back, he saw Cypriot infantry troops with two ageing T-34 tanks heading east along the coastal road. Alex was thinking, *They are heading to Six-mile Beach; it's the only beach large enough to accommodate an amphibious assault.*

After leaving the loaded car with Danielle and their two kids, Alex ran to the post office to make another call to Akrotiri. He got the Vice-Admiral, who shouted, 'I thought you were on leave?'

Alex apologised, asked for further information about the invasion force and said, 'They have two ageing torpedo-boats in the harbour. I am not sure whether the Cypriots are using them for an attack but I spoke to the commanding officer a couple of days ago. He said they were short of qualified seamen but explained that the boats were okay. I want to give them a hand.' The line went silent but Alex could hear the Vice-Admiral breathing.

'If you do that, you are on your own,' he said and hung up.

Alex rushed back to Danielle and their kids and said, 'Please, take the kids west of town and wait. Be prepared to evacuate westward along the coast to Myrtou, then to Morphou and via Xeros-Lefka to Troodos. There is no other way. We can't get over the range to Nicosia; the Turks are there.'

'What are you going to do?' Danielle asked anxiously.

'Wait for me but move out if the shooting starts here. I have something more to do.'

Alex grabbed his gear bag from the booth, kissed Danielle and his children. 'You are coming with us, aren't you, Dad?' William said with a nervous voice.

'Don't worry, be strong and take care of your mum and sister. I will be with you soon,' Alex answered as he darted down the road towards the Kyrenia castle.

At the castle, he found the Commanding officer at the two boats. His name was Janie. Alex learned that he was a volunteer because he had been a sailor in the merchant navy all his active life. There was only him and two young soldiers. 'Are you going to engage the Turks?' Alex asked.

'I have no orders and everybody is heading towards Six-mile Beach. I will like to go.'

'That's fine,' Alex said. 'I am a British Naval Officer; if you allow, I will help you.'

'I reckoned that,' Janie said with a wry smile.

The two young soldiers nervously joined the two men on one of the boats, where Alex explained his strategy. 'We have four torpedos, two on each vessel. When released towards a target, there is no need to hang on, so get out as quickly as you can. You boys will operate the heavy machine guns on the deck and fire on command against our target. We will attack landing vessels only. Follow my command and we will be okay. Now, arm the machine guns.' The two soldiers quickly dragged bands of ammunition to the two machine guns and prepared to fire. Alex and Janie checked the torpedo tubes and the release mechanisms. Alex activated all four torpedoes.

Janie and Alex started the two boat's heavy diesel engines, sending a black pillar of smoke upwards in a roar. Alex looked up at the castle and saw Batzev looking over the wall, probably wondering what was going on. He waved as they cast off and slowly sailed out of the narrow harbour channel, one by one.

31

The boats were responsive to the throttle and relatively fast. Alex was in front, followed by Janie, who steered as close as he could to Alex's stern, so with the spray it would be difficult for an enemy to recognise more than one vessel. Unfortunately, the soldier at the heavy machine gun got drenched.

As they sailed forward, they spotted the invasion fleet. To Alex's surprise, a corvette size vessel had split away from the fleet and headed towards them. He recognised the vessel as a Flower-class corvette from WWII, equipped with anti-aircraft guns. Alex decided to attack. He grabbed the radio microphone and gave his command to Janie, who diverted to his starboard and caught up. Alex caught the attention of Janie and with two hands indicating that they should attack from two sides. It would be more difficult said than done. The Corvette had little horizontal firepower and sailed straight at them. He could see that the crew tried to lower the twin machine gun on the foredeck as the two torpedo-boats came closer. Alex ordered the machine gun to fire. The two boats diverted fast, one to starboard and the other to port. It was a risky move but his machine gunner was quick and Alex could hear projectiles flying, removing the foredeck crew on the

Corvette. Alex took a sharp turn, raising a wave and steered the torpedo-boat towards the Corvette's side. He could not see Janie. Alex's boat came under heavy machine-gun fire but the soldier on the deck replied with small bursts of precise fire. When they were close enough, Alex released the starboard torpedo. The Corvette turned rapidly and he released the port side torpedo. Alex could barely see what happened to his torpedoes but saw the first one missing its target. Then he heard the soldier at the machine-gun shouting, 'It's coming!' and a large explosion followed, raising a tall pillar of water up alongside the Corvette. Yet another explosion followed on the other side of the vessel. Instantly, the Corvette stopped and Alex thought that they had hit the engine room. He grabbed the microphone to the radio and shouted, 'Abandon, abandon.'

The two torpedo-boats met up to estimate their damage. There were bullet holes everywhere and Alex's boat took in water. Alex said over the radio, 'Let's tie up.' Janie came alongside and quickly they tied the two boats together forward, mid-ships across and after. Alex promptly explained, 'We still have two more torpedos aboard but we cannot arm the tubes; the torpedoes are too heavy. Let's activate them and steer right towards the centre of the invasion fleet. We lock the wheel on the port boat and steer with the starboard one. When we are within range, we lock the wheel, hoping that the boats will stay on course. Then we all jump overboard. I have four sets of underwater breathing devices to stay below the surface for a short while. Be aware, Jets are coming in.' Alex did not think that Janie had fully understood but time was short and he instructed to fire the engines up. Slowly the boats rose to half planning and he gave the signal to full throttle.

The water in the hull slowed them down but Alex was happy with the speed. He commanded Janie and his soldier to climb over, using hand signals, so that all four were in the same boat. Just before they were close enough, he handed a small breathing device to Janie and the soldiers.

'When in the water, open the valve and breath but only if you see an aircraft approaching. Drop your lifejackets and swim like hell. The aircraft will shoot at the lifejackets.' Alex took a hand grenade out of his kit and taped it to a post in the cabin. He quickly tied a thin fishing line from the safety-split through the door opening, closing it from outside. He tied the fishing line to the latch, hiding the knot between the wall and the door—a perfect trap. Alex saw the mass of the invasion fleet in the distance and locked the last rudder. They all jumped overboard.

Machine-gun fire ran through the water and passed the four men closely. Alex shouted, 'He is coming back, drop the lifejackets and dive.' A minute later, they could from below see machine-gun fire ripping through the floating lifejackets. They swam until the breathing gas ran out and continued swimming on the surface towards the shore. Alex and Janie had trouble following the two young soldiers. They walked barefooted ashore onto a narrow strip of sand between rocky outcrops. They could hear the sounds of artillery and machine-gun fire less than a mile away. Alex got up and said, 'We better get going.' At that moment, a massive explosion and a pillar of fire reached up among the vessels further from the beach.

Later they arrived back in Kyrenia and Alex told Janie and the two soldiers to go to their families and get out of town, following the coastal road to Morphou. They parted and Alex walked as fast he could towards the West, where he thought that Danielle and their two children waited. Bombs had damaged the town, and there were still planes in the air.

Crawling over falling walls and through alleys, he slowly moved forward until he reached a white military UN vehicle with a large UN flag flying from the antenna. In front, there was a long row of civilian cars as far as he could see. The cars were loaded with people and with luggage on the roof. 'Where on earth is Danielle and the kids?' he asked himself. Alex stopped next to the UN vehicle to catch his breath when he felt someone tapping on his head. He looked up and to his surprise saw the face of Lisa. She was in camouflage uniform, carrying a handgun only.

'We are waiting for you,' she said with a smile. The UN people evacuated by helicopter; they left their vehicles behind. We had to organise a convoy. She grabbed a microphone and said, 'He is here.'

'Run to the front,' Lisa said.

'Three more families are coming,' Alex said, mobilising his reserve strength and started to run on sore feet. He didn't realise how thirsty he was. He passed two Guardians with M16's before reaching the convoy front.

Alex, at first, did not believe what he saw. In the front was a UN open vehicle similar to the one in the back. On the passenger side was an officer in camouflage uniform looking forward with binoculars. On her shoulder straps were a gold band across, indicating the rank of lieutenant, but attached was a tricolour rosette in blue, red and white, and in the middle a Scarlet Pimpernel. The officer turned around and looked at Alex. He had found his wife, Danielle. She bent over the side of the vehicle, kissed him on the forehead and said,

'Our kids are in the car, you take the wheel.' She pointed at the car behind, where their two kids were trying to get his attention through an open window. Danielle gave the hand signal for moving forward. It travelled between the two Guardians to Rita in the back of the convoy. Slowly they moved forward.

The column travelled at a low speed. There was a constant fear of Turkish planes that had dropped bombs at random. Everybody hoped that the UN flag would prevent a further bombing. Still, both Lisa and Danielle knew the reason for the evacuation of UN personnel was that Turkey no longer supported the deployment of the UN in the northern part of Cyprus. As the convoy drove forward, people were anxiously looking for incoming planes. Nobody could hear them before they had passed and it was just to wait for the explosion. But nothing happened. Alex had been scanning the slopes of the Kyrenia Mountains and had seen, with satisfaction, bursts of laser light emitted against the incoming planes. *The experimental gadget worked*, he thought, *but only for now.* Soon the aircraft would realise that their enemy had not fired laser-guided missiles. Alex felt that the progression of the convoy was painstakingly slow but he knew well that this would always be the case. The convoy had to stop many times to assist broken-down cars. At the Six-mile Beach, the Turkish planes were busy. Flying along the coast depended on the fuel the aircraft had left before returning to Turkey. It was a relief when the convoy reached Myrtou. Now the road was downhill and flat over the Morphou plain to Lefka. They encountered many refugees in broken-down vehicles and long military convoys.

It was dark when the convoy reached the relative safety of Troodos. On the back seat, William and Josephine had been fast asleep for a couple of hours. When the convoy stopped, Alex rushed out of the car and caught up with Danielle, who was busy organising parking for the convoy in the narrow streets. They had to spend the night in Troodos before proceeding to Limassol, where a makeshift refugee camp was established. It was too dangerous to drive at night.

Danielle ran towards Alex and the car with their children. Short in breath, she stuttered, 'I got a message that at 10 PM, the Turkish Cypriot militia in Paphos has surrendered. I suggest you immediately drive with Josephine and William to Villa Yanni and stay there until I have finished this job—it should be safe.'

Alex embraced Danielle and said, 'Take care of yourself, darling.'

He jumped into the car and heard Danielle saying, 'You better take care of our kids.'

'Aye, aye, Sir,' he replied and drove off. Danielle watched the car disappearing down the road among the vineyards.

Alex arrived late at night at Villa Yanni. Erik was in the villa and was eager to hear any news of Lisa and the general situation. He had tried to contact the Danish UN command in Morphou to get information but his previous brothers-in-arms had little to give him. They offered him refuge in the Lefka camp, which Erik politely declined.

When Alex had fed his children and put them to bed, he realised how tired and dirty he was. His clothes had dried but Erik was quick to point out that he smelled like a zoo, which both William and Josephine complained about when they were in the car. He had a shower and a change of clothes and joined Erik on the upstairs veranda.

The two men sat in silence, looking out into the night. There were only a few lights and they could hear random gunfire in the direction of Limassol. Alex ate only a little and the Metaxa brandy Erik had offered him quickly went to his head. Alex asked Erik about the whereabouts of Avo and Dewan and got the answers he already knew; Avo supported troops in Nicosia and Dewan was in the UN headquarters in Nicosia Airport. 'So, what did you do in Kyrenia—did you go diving on your own?' Erik asked.

Alex smiled and said, 'As a matter of fact, I did.'

'Tell me all about it,' Erik asked while pouring himself another brandy. He looked at Alex and said, 'Sorry, please help yourself.' Alex was not in a hurry, leaned back in the armchair and looked up in the veranda roof. Although he had tried while driving in convoy, he had not yet sorted out the morning's events. His mind was on his children's well-being.

'I thought that I had to do something,' Alex said. 'The Turks were landing at Six-mile Beach.'

'There were two torpedo-boats in the harbour,' Alex continued, 'the Commander, Janie, and I thought that we should entertain the Turks. We managed to sink a couple of boats before we went for a swim. It went all right. We had two young soldiers with us; they were good but they out-swam us on the way to the shore.'

'Did that matter?' Erik asked.

'No,' Alex answered, 'but it was depressing; I think I am ready to join you in retirement.' Erik laughed.

Erik and Alex did not hear from Lisa and Danielle for another three days until they both showed up in one of the UN vehicles they "borrowed" in Kyrenia. They did not look exhausted and their uniforms were clean. Erik could not keep his Nordic sarcasm at bay and said, 'What hotel did you stay in?' He did not get an answer, not even a shrug.

Danielle and Lisa stayed in Villa Yanni on and off but spent a lot of time in the Troodos Mountains. The fighting continued for three weeks, mostly further away.

A rare phone call came through to Villa Yanni; it was Dewan. He explained that fighting around the UN headquarters in Nicosia Airport had been fierce, forcing most UN personnel to evacuate for Limassol. He asked Alex whether it was possible to pick him up. He needed a break.

Alex returned to Villa Yanni with Dewan and both Danielle and Lisa had come down from the Troodos Mountains. When Lisa saw Dewan, her first reaction was, 'I will suggest that you borrow one of Erik's suits while I get the one you wear to the dry-cleaner.' Dewan had lost weight and was exhausted. He was happy for Lisa's offer, which Erik applauded because he did not wear suits anymore.

Later, Kamal Bashour arrived. He had flown in from Egypt just before the Coup D'état and had stayed at the Chrysorroyiatissa Monastery. He had been appointed as the Coptic Church envoy to the Vatican and had prepared himself for his new job. He handed over a white envelope with the Coptic Church insignia to Danielle. She opened the envelope and read a card. 'Alex,' she said, 'we are invited to an audience with His Beatitude Archbishop Makarios III tomorrow; he is in the Monastery.'

'That's a surprise but interesting,' Alex responded.

They all sat down at the upstairs veranda, enjoying the afternoon sea breeze after a warm day. They were silent because the previous events had been complex and tragic. Nobody wanted to start the conversation. They enjoyed the fresh fruit, bread and wine on offer.

Dewan appeared freshly showered in one of Erik's suits, sat down, looked at Kamal and said, 'I have spoken to Mauritz Batzev. When the Turks conquered Kyrenia, an officer immediately arrested him and took away Alexander's vessel. After two days in the police detention in Kyrenia, Mauritz was released and ordered to stay inside the Kyrenia Castle. The US President had to intervene, forcing the Turks to release him but they would not hand the vessel back. I have made further enquiries. As I understand it, the vessel is in Ankara under the protection of the Ministry of Antiquities.'

Dewan paused and looked at Alex and said, 'Through a third person, I informed the current ruler of Oman, Qaboos bin Said that the Pearl of Allah was in the hands of Turkey. It did not take long before the Imam of Mecca requested the pearl to be handed over to the Mosque in Muscat. A war of words broke out between the Prime minister of Turkey, Bülent Ecevit and Sultan Qaboos bin Said.' Dewan paused, enjoying his audience suspense.

He slowly sipped his wine. Dewan continued, 'The result was that in the end they reached an agreement. The religious authorities will negotiate the fate of the pearl before the Fatwa can be withdrawn.'

Alex leaned back in his armchair and laughed. Everybody was looking at him. He looked back and realised that he had to explain. 'Back in Akrotiri, I walked down the corridor in the headquarters and passed one of my agents who smiled wryly and said: Lucky you, on vacation, huh, I hear that you have successfully placed a sleeper agent in Ankara. I thought that it was some wry joke and let it pass. Now I know better.'

Alex explained, 'You may not all know but I replaced the pearl of Alexander with an artificial pearl. As you know, the real pearl of Alexander was an intended offering to Aphrodite and that is where it belongs. London made the artificial one using a newly developed combustion agent called Thermite. It consists of aluminium nanoparticles, which increases the aluminium surface area, coated with passivating iron oxide. The compound is embedded in a polymer. It is designed to combust after a three-second delay activated by the combustion of magnesium strips. The polymer sphere is coated with nacre, giving it the appearance of a natural pearl. Moving the pearl up and down in its cradle twice will ignite a magnesium strip. It is swift and hot combustion, allowing the pearl to melt completely. It is like firing a large photographic flashbulb.'

Kamal looked at Alex, shook his head and said, 'What a thing to do; I took the pearl out only once and quickly put it back because I realised it was a fake.'

With an assuring smile, Alex said, 'The pearl will combust into gasses. Nothing will be left; that's the whole point.' The room was silent.

Then Dewan raised his glass and said, 'Cheers to that.'

A few days later, Alex drove to Akrotiri, where he handed in his resignation. He was disappointed with the lack of engagement by Britain, so lightly carving into US demands. To him, it was clear that the inactivity had worsened the crisis. The Vice-Admiral looked at him and said, 'Do not do this in haste, Alex; I will keep your resignation until you return to London, then we can discuss the matter.' Alex was not in the mood for a serious discussion and accepted the decision. The Vice-Admiral added, 'I am too busy writing my resignation.'

The next day, The United Nations Security Council Resolution 360 was adopted. The council declared its respect for the Republic of Cyprus' sovereignty, independence and territorial integrity and recorded its formal disapproval of the unilateral military actions taken against it by Turkey. It was said that the Minister of Foreign Affairs of Turkey was laughing when he left the UN building in New York.

Ingram Content Group UK Ltd.
Milton Keynes UK
UKHW020621170523
421882UK00009B/148

9 781398 470590